BATTLE for WHITEROCK

Jeff Miller

First Edition, 2025

ISBN: 978-1-64590-071-9

Published by Kingdom Winds Publishing.
www.kingdomwinds.com
publishing@kingdomwinds.com
Printed in the United States of America.

Special thanks to Joyce Magnin for all of your patience and hard work helping coach this rookie writer and to Codi and the Kingdom Winds team for making this dream of mine a reality.

Dedicated to the loving memory of my parents, whose constant support will never be forgotten.

Jeff Miller

ONE

A frigid sting whipped across Aiden's face as he soared above the trees on his red and gold-scaled commonlear dragon. He breathed in the sweet scent of fallen leaves as the rising sun pierced through the fog below and onto the marvelous late-autumn colors strewn across his father's kingdom.

In just a short time, Aiden spotted the clearing in the woods where he was to meet his two fellow squires, his best friends.

"It looks like Aeric beat us here, gal," Aiden said as he patted Lucy on her neck. "If my eyes are seeing through that fog all right, it looks like a brown and gold commonlear down there."

Lucy snorted in affirmation and swooped down.

"Yes, that's Aeric's dragon all right." Aiden peered around for other commonlears. "I wonder if Samuel and Zachariah are here yet."

Lucy burst through the covering of fog and made a swift and steady landing next to her counterpart, Cameron.

Lucy snorted and nodded, and Cameron returned the greeting likewise.

"Greetings, Aiden. Good to see you," Aiden heard from behind as he took off his riding gloves. He turned around. Walking from the center of the field with a bright smile on his face was his father's chief advisor and the kingdom's second in command, Sir Zachariah. "It looks like the fog will clear just in time," he said.

Zachariah's long gray cloak almost matched the color of his hair and beard. Beneath that beard, Aiden noticed a face that was showing signs of age. More wrinkles had formed around his eyes, and his leathery skin was starting to sag a bit. But a rugged handsomeness hadn't fully left Zachariah yet. The king's chief advisor rubbed his hands together as his warm breath swirled in the chilly morning air.

"Good morning, Sir Zachariah," Aiden said. "Good to see you, too."

Before Aiden or Zachariah could get in another word, Aiden heard a voice to his side.

"Still up to the challenge, Aiden?" Aeric walked toward Aiden with his arms folded and head cocked.

"Of course!" Aiden replied as he sprung off Lucy.

"Good," Aeric said. "You know, I've been thinking. We haven't discussed what the loser will owe the winner. How about good old-fashioned humiliation?"

Aiden lifted an eyebrow and smirked. "I'm up for that."

"Good. The loser gets to squire for the winner for a day. Can you imagine? The son of the king being *my* servant for a *whole* day?"

Aiden chuckled. "You know as well as I do—that's not gonna happen. But what about the guy who comes in second?"

"Oh, you mean Samuel? Well, I say the middle guy gets nothing either way."

"Okay, fine with me, so long as Samuel goes for it."

Just as Aiden uttered those words, a shimmering, black-scaled dragon swiftly broke through the fog and landed next to the brown and gold Cameron. They greeted each other with a few friendly snorts.

"Good day, Grandfather," Samuel said to Zachariah. "I made it."

"I see that." Zachariah smiled. "I thought you were right behind me."

"Well, I was," Samuel said as he dismounted Savannah. "It helps when you bring your bows and arrows to the test. Had to go back and get them."

Zachariah laughed, shook his head, and gave a firm clap. "Everyone ready now?"

"I'm ready," Aiden replied with a chuckle.

"Yes, me too," Aeric said, also laughing at Samuel's gaffe.

"Then let's start." Zachariah turned toward Whiterock Mountain, shielded his eyes from the sun still burning through the fog, and pointed to the nearby forest between them and the mountain. "You have to fly through the forest, zooming through the trees as fast as you can, and then enter Whiterock Canyon and hit targets there, dotted all the way up to the top of Whiterock Mountain. You have to fly and shoot. No slowing down. Did you remember to bring your colored quills?"

"Yes," they all said.

"Good. That's the only way I'll know who shot what," Zachariah said with a smile. "Aiden, Aeric, your fathers and I will meet you at the conclusion of the test at the top of the mountain. Before we start, let's say a quick prayer."

Aiden squirmed. He didn't like prayers; they were ridiculous and outdated. Didn't anyone realize they never worked? But he didn't want to make a fuss about it in front of everyone. He bowed his head with his fellow squires, kept his mouth shut, and after enduring the brief prayer, he was on his way with his young blood brothers toward their dragons.

This is it, Aiden thought as he placed his riding gloves back on. *The moment I've been waiting for all my life. Knighthood. I couldn't be more ready.*

As the three squires mounted their dragons, Aiden nodded to Samuel, who returned the nod. Aiden smirked at Aeric, who smirked back. The three dragons extended their wings, rose to their feet, hovered over the ground, and turned to face Zachariah. Their trainer raised his hand and held it there. Aiden's heart pounded as he involuntarily held his breath. Zachariah quickly lowered his hand, and the steeds were off.

Samuel and Savannah dashed off before Lucy and Cameron could get a good start.

"What the…?" Aiden dug his heels into Lucy's sides. She sped ahead of Aeric well enough, and it didn't take long for Aiden to catch up to Samuel.

"I can't let you win!" Aiden yelled.

"What?" Samuel said. "Oh, wait! I forgot about the race!" Samuel smiled and dug his heels harder into Savannah. They sped off even faster.

"Why you little…" And Lucy knew what to do. Aiden and Lucy flew faster, with Aeric and Cameron trailing not far behind.

The three young lads had practiced their maneuvers through the forest hundreds of times—and so had their commonlears. It didn't matter which path they took; the boys and their commonlears were in sync, zooming through the trees, weaving in and out, as if they had every branch memorized.

Aiden felt an exhilaration well up inside him, and he knew Lucy felt it too. She was flying faster than she ever had before, with the precision and skill she had perfected.

Aiden looked about. Samuel was quite a distance to his left, but only ahead by the length of a commonlear, if that. Aeric, on the other hand…

"Where *is* Aeric?" Aiden asked Lucy. She snorted as if she didn't care, and Aiden shrugged his shoulders. Within a moment, Aiden saw Aeric catch up on his right.

"It's about time you showed up!" Aiden yelled.

Aeric yelled back something incoherent, probably derogatory. Aiden ignored it.

It wasn't long before they shot out of the forest like darts. They passed through another clearing that led to the creek. They followed Spring Creek to a magnificent waterfall that flowed within a crescent break of the rocky mountainside. The dragons arched over the top of the falls, gained momentum, and zoomed along the running stream straight into the gorge.

In the distance, an enormous red blur caught their attention.

"Did you see that?" Samuel shouted. "What was that thing? A dragon? I've never seen anything like that."

As soon as Samuel let those words out, a swift sound and chilling breeze sent shivers up Aiden's spine. His back straightened. His stomach tightened.

"Something's coming."

All three squires turned around just in time to see what it was—a giant, red man-wolf with wings. Its hairy, bulging arms lunged out for them.

"Split up!" Aiden yelled.

The commonlears flew in opposite directions as the worgraith lunged. Its claw-like feet found footing along the canyon wall just ahead, and the worgraith sprung itself off for another attack.

Lucy dove behind a rock in the thick of the forest above the gorge, and Savannah flew behind a boulder along the creek. But Cameron was soaring madly, still spooked by the hideous creature. The red worgraith easily eyed the frantic commonlear and his rider, who was anxiously trying to calm his dragon to gain control.

"Cameron, Cameron, come on!" Aeric screamed. "Cameron… *dear God!*"

Aeric let go of Cameron's reigns to draw an arrow. Cameron's panicky flight nearly threw Aeric off. Before Aeric could fire his bow, the dragon rushed in. It thrust out its mighty hand and snatched Cameron and Aeric.

Aiden sat frozen in his hiding place. He felt the earth spin. Tears welled in his eyes. But it didn't take long for his mourning to turn into rage. Aiden dug his heels into Lucy's sides, and she charged.

"Over here!" Aiden waved, bow and arrow still in hand. He whistled. "Over here, you mangy, no-good mutt! Come and get me!" Aiden pulled his bow and watched the worgraith quickly turn around. "Come on, right between his eyes," he said softly as Lucy charged the beast like a jouster. …*that's it… never mind your fear, never mind what you see in its hand…*

The worgraith bowed its head low as it kept its beady eyes fixed on Aiden. It rolled back its mouth, bearing its sharp yellow teeth and dark gums. Saliva dripped from the sides of its mouth. As it slowly let out a deep growl, a billowy cloud of dark smoke wafted out of the cracks between its teeth.

Lucy screeched and took off, nearly throwing Aiden from his saddle.

"Lucy!" Aiden yelled, "Wait! *NO!*"

Lucy flew back toward the waterfalls. Aiden looked back. The worgraith spread its wings, picked itself up, and charged. But a buzzing movement making its way toward the beast caught Aiden's eye. It was Savannah and Samuel.

Savannah flew above the worgraith as Samuel pelted the dragon with arrows as fast as he could. The brute turned upwards to Samuel. In one hand it still clenched the limp forms of Aeric and Cameron, while the other hand tried to ward off Samuel, but Savannah flew high enough and out of its way.

"Lucy, arch back. We need to help Samuel and Savannah!"

Hearing their names and their need for help was all it took for Lucy to find her courage again. She circled as fast as she could. Soon, the two fighters pelted the worgraith with arrows as their dragons buzzed like hornets around the beast. The immense dragon tried to swat against the stinging arrows while it picked itself up and chased them abruptly through the curving, narrow gorge. Savannah found the opportunity to dig her sharp talons into the top of the worgraith's head. The worgraith roared as it tried to shake Savannah off. This forced her to dig her claws deeper into its skull as she tried her best to hang on.

"Savannah!" Samuel yelled. "Let go! I can't hang on…" Just above the waterfalls, the beast smacked Savannah off, which flung Samuel into the air, and he tumbled downward in front of the waterfall and into the rocky pool below.

"No! Samuel!" Horrified, Aiden watched the fate of his second blood brother. Aiden choked back the tears swelling in his eyes. His mind spun again. His eyes searched to the pool for Samuel. Aiden's concentration broke when he heard the worgraith crash into the wall of the gorge above the waterfall. He spun around just in time to witness the beast, slightly shaken by the hit, snag Savannah in midair.

Aiden couldn't move. He and Lucy just hovered there, watching, without a thought to even move out of sight.

But the still-dazed worgraith didn't even notice Aiden. It lifted itself up and took off.

"We'll come back for vengeance," he said to Lucy. "He will *not* get away with this!"

It was suddenly eerily silent. No birds. No wind. Nothing. It seemed as if even the clouds gave up their movement.

I can't believe it. Aiden thought. So suddenly. First Aeric, then Samuel. What…just…happened?

Lucy squawked and beat her wings faster. "Lucy! What are you…?" She flew a few paces down the creek. "SAMUEL! He's alive!"

As they flew in closer, Aiden saw his best friend pull himself onto the shore in great pain. He could barely maneuver himself just a few feet to sit up against a large standing rock.

Before Lucy had both feet down on the pebbly shore, Aiden had jumped off her back and ran to Samuel. By that time, Samuel's head slumped against his chest.

Aiden grabbed his friend's shoulders and tried not to shake too hard. "Samuel, Samuel, can you hear me?" Battered, bruised, and bloodied, Samuel didn't reply. Aiden hadn't noticed any broken bones, but he feared there might be internal damage.

He whistled for Lucy and nodded for her to come close. "We're going to get these worgraiths," Aiden said to Samuel. "I don't know if you can hear me, but we are going to *get* these things. If it's the last thing we do, I swear. It's not over. For what they did to you, to …Aeric—"

Aiden pushed Samuel's torso forward, squeezed himself between Samuel and the rock, and lifted him up. Aiden dragged Samuel a few feet, hoping he wasn't adding to any internal damage, and with care, he slowly heaved Samuel face-down across Lucy's back, just in front of her saddle.

"I've got nothing to keep Samuel secure, so we'll have to fly carefully. Are you ready?"

Lucy snorted, and Aiden mounted. He gave her a cluck, and she unfurled her wings for takeoff. But Lucy stopped just short and cocked her head skyward.

"Lucy, what…" Aiden began, fearing an oncoming worgraith. He heard flapping commonlear wings and voices. They were men, and they were frantically calling the names of Samuel, Aeric, and Aiden.

"Over here!" Aiden yelled with a mix of urgency and relief. His voice was shaky.

Aiden caught sight of his father, King Jared; Samuel's grandfather, Zachariah; and Aeric's father, Sir Franklin. The moment was a mixture of elation and wretched horror. Aiden's head spun, and his heart sank. He suddenly felt nausea mixed with a tightened anxiety. How was he going to tell Aeric's father the news of his only son's horrific death?

"Aiden!" his father shouted.

Aeric's father cried out, "Aeric! Aiden, is Aeric here?"

Aiden just looked down and waited for them to land. Without hesitation, Zachariah jumped off his dragon and ran for Samuel.

"He's all right," Aiden confirmed, seeing the look on Zachariah's face.

"Aeric. Where is Aeric?" Sir Franklin asked, his face a mask of shock and confusion. Sir Franklin's eyes displayed his struggle to find hope.

Turning to Zachariah, Aiden said, "I was about to take Samuel—"

"I'll take him from here," Zachariah interrupted.

Lucy lay down and allowed Zachariah to take Samuel.

"Where is Aeric?"

Aiden again ignored Sir Franklin as he watched Zachariah lift Samuel, offering no help to the elder. Aiden couldn't think; he couldn't move.

"Aiden," King Jared gently asked, "Where is Aeric?"

Aiden forced himself to look at his father, but he could not bear to look at Sir Franklin. "He died, father; I'm sorry…" Aiden could no longer hold back the tears.

Aiden was only two years old when worgraiths were last in Whiterock. That was sixteen years ago, just months before his sister was born. He had never fully heard the story of the last attack. He had only known that many people had died, including Samuel's father, who fought against it as a knight.

King Jared broke the silence. "It brings back memories," he said. "Horrible ones."

The three had been on the pebbly shore, astride their dragons, for what might have been just a short time. Or long... Aiden couldn't quite tell.

"I just...I just wish I was there when this happened," Sir Franklin said as he smacked his fist into his saddle. "To protect my son...or at least try...I was so close, just up the mountain. Had I known. I could have ...*should* have been there to prevent his death."

Sir Franklin wiped a few tears, and through his wobbly voice eked out, "I could have been the one who died instead of him...and now...I can't even see his face one last time." He punched into his saddle again. He held his fist to his lips to stifle a wail.

King Jared spoke to him softly, tears streaming down his face as well. "It wasn't your fault."

Sir Franklin didn't respond.

"Go home. Grieve in peace," King Jared said. "Aiden and I will attend to calling our knights. We will plan a mission to hunt down these monsters—again."

Sir Franklin could not stifle a bitter wail. He raised his tightened fist from his mouth and shook it as if to strike his saddle again, but then he dropped it as if all his strength had left him.

After a moment, Sir Franklin said, "And I will go with you. I swear I will hunt every single one of these things down myself if I have to."

King Jared made no reply to Sir Franklin, but nodded to Aiden as he whipped Enoch's reins and led the three out of the canyon.

By the time they had neared the village at Whiterock, it was alive with bustle and excitement. Underneath the thatched roofs, smith shops were in full production; carts full of goods moved in and out of the open village gates. Traders shouted their wares, and crowds milled about. Some children chased each other in the streets while others stood enamored by a juggler tossing flaming torches in the air.

Not a single one knows the horrifying thing that had happened just a brief flight away, Aiden thought. *...they have no idea what treacherous monster, or monsters, could make its way to the village if we don't respond soon.*

King Jared, Sir Franklin, and Aiden hovered overhead. By this time, Aiden had expected to be joining Aeric and Samuel in celebrating their success as his father publicly announced that he would dub them as knights.

King Jared peered over at Sir Franklin. "My friend, this is where we part, for now. Go home, and may God be with you and your family. Our prayers are with you."

Sir Franklin looked back toward Whiterock Gorge. "Yes," he said, with barely any strength left. "Please, call on my service; I will not be in too mournful of a state to fight. Trust me; it would better my spirits to seek revenge on these things."

"Please," King Jared replied. "I insist. Stay at home instead. Be a comfort to your wife. I will call upon the knights garrisoned in your land."

"No, my king," Sir Franklin said. "I will call them to your castle for battle. It will be my honor."

"As you wish," King Jared replied.

Without a word, Sir Franklin turned his commonlear and headed westward past the village and into the shire of Benaria where he lorded.

King Jared watched him for a moment and then glanced at Aiden as he commanded his commonlear, Enoch, to move on. Aiden followed. He glanced once again behind him—at the gorge and then to Whiterock Mountain. It seemed so peaceful now.

Whiterock Mountain stretched skyward, as if it were yearning to reach Heaven. It appeared as if it had no desire to expand itself along the horizon as most of Whiterock's mountains wanted to do. Instead, it seemed as if it had, at some point in the beginning of time, victoriously staked its claim as the king of mountains. Perhaps the great monolith gathered the courage to rise higher because it had something that no other Whiterock mountain had: a unique natural phenomenon—its peak was not the whitest snow anyone had ever seen but the whitest marble anyone had ever seen, thus lending itself, and the kingdom, its name.

Aiden turned away from the mountain and looked ahead at his home, Whiterock Palace. Despair left him for a moment as he tugged on Lucy's reins. She gently swept downward toward home. It was as peaceful and delightful as ever.

Whiterock palace was almost a mountain unto itself, composed of neatly arranged towers, both big and small, spreading both upward and outward. The king's personal chambers soared far above the castle's other towers. Outbuildings included an infirmary and royal stables. The neatly landscaped grounds offered plenty of field space behind the castle to host various tournaments, with space left over to house tents for participating knights. A spring-fed moat surrounded the castle grounds.

Except for some of the world's finest redwood imported from Rosendra, slate imported from Dyria to grace the roof, and granite mined in Whiterock's San Lira Granite Quarry to form its foundation, Whiterock Palace was built entirely out of Whiterock Mountain's marble. And there was plenty of it throughout the mountain. Not only was the marble at the mountain's peak, but it visibly veined here and there down the mountainside and occasionally weaved itself throughout the gorge.

The further down the mountain the veins went, the more color corrupted the white marble, but that was no problem. Well-paid workers mined the marble, pure white and colored, and hoisted the marble onto heavy flats that dragons then flew to the castle's small island.

The castle was an engineering marvel that took years to construct. It wasn't just the general building that took time, but well-known sculptors from neighboring kingdoms crafted every hallway arch and pillar. They chipped away to make intricate statues and reliefs for its walls and vaulted ceilings and tracery within its windows. Artisans had carved the tables, chairs, and the floor from the colored marble with exquisite attention to detail. Painters from all over came to portray religious and historical images on select ceilings and walls. By the time the castle was complete, it had become the greatest man-made marvel of the known world.

The colored marble also marked the stables, infirmary, walkways, and the arch that bridged the village at Whiterock to the castle island.

As Aiden and King Jared descended, the busy people at the castle stopped their work and looked skyward. They ran to the returning party, some waving their hands and shouting congratulations, their faces beaming with delight.

Again, if things had panned out as they were supposed to, Aiden would have arrived with Aeric and Samuel, and with Zachariah and Sir Franklin, and all would have been celebrating together. He tried his best to stretch a smile across his face and lift his hand to wave hello.

The dragons landed softly as the party of congratulators hushed and bowed.

Aiden could tell that his father needed a moment to gather his voice and his courage to say what was needful to say. "You may rise," the king said.

Giving them a moment to do so, the king continued. "My citizens," he declared from his commonlear. "I know all of you were planning on seeing my son and his fellow squires earn their knighthood today. But…I'm afraid there has been an accident." King Jared stopped as his mouth quivered and his eyes filled with tears. The crowd remained silent. "It seems Samuel has been badly injured…"

Aiden looked down into the crowd; and judging from their appearance, apparently Zachariah had brought Samuel directly to the infirmary. His eyes landed for the first time that day on his sixteen-year-old sister, Alicia. The proud and excited smile on her face turned to alarm with the rest of the well-wishers.

Alicia was the spitting image of their mother—beautiful green eyes paired with thick, curly red-blond hair that cascaded down her warm and gentle face and below her shoulders. She was graceful and sweet, without a care in the world. She loved to laugh, and her smile lit her entire face.

Aiden didn't want her to hear this. She was so innocent.

"…perhaps even fatally so," the king continued. "It is hard to tell at this point. Sir Zachariah has taken him to the recovery center. Possibly, with your prayers, Samuel will regain his health." King Jared paused and looked downward. With red, tear-filled eyes, he took a deep breath and, with an almost broken voice, said, "Aeric… is dead."

As one, the crowd gasped as a scattering of whispers filled the air. Many covered their faces to hide their mourning.

"He died…" King Jared hung his head as his lips quivered. "Ladies and gentlemen…Aeric died tragically during the test." He left it at that. As King Jared dismounted his dragon, he let a tear fall. The crowd bowed low and made room to allow their king passage.

Puzzled, Aiden whispered, "Father," but apparently not loud enough.

King Jared took Enoch's reins and walked him to his stable. The commonlear usually walked behind its master with head held high, back straight, and legs in solid step. But today, even Enoch's body slumped a bit. He held his head low and moved his legs in a sullen lumber.

Aiden didn't want to draw attention. He knew his father must have had a reason for not saying how Aeric had died, but under the dire circumstances, no reason could be good enough. They had a right to know for their own safety. Perhaps even to evacuate.

Aiden roused from his musings. The servants were still silently bowing, waiting for him to dismount and follow his father. Aiden did so and tried to hurry to his father's side to address him. But a worried, incessant voice interrupted him.

"Aiden, are you alright? What happened?"

Aiden held back his petulance. He knew he couldn't take out his feelings on Alicia. He looked over his shoulder. People were still close by. Some were staring. "I'm alright," he said with soft frustration.

"Aiden, what…what went on? What happened?" Alicia's face wrinkled.

Aiden replied in a hushed voice, teeth clenched, "I'll tell you later. In private. Right now, I need to talk with Father."

Aiden glanced around. The people were quietly and worriedly talking among themselves over the apparent news. He knew everyone within earshot; they were castle staff. They were like family, but at that moment, he wished they were gone. Aiden turned and walked Lucy into her stable. Alicia followed.

"I wish you would say something."

Aiden turned. "I realize, Alicia, you have the right to know. Aeric and Samuel are nearly brothers to you, too." Not able to look directly at her, Aiden added, "I told you. I will tell you later—privately."

Alicia glared. Then, without a word, she spun around and walked off.

Aiden walked into the stables. After securing the doors, he stopped short of bellowing for his father.

A stable boy approached, and King Jared handed him Enoch's reins. "I know my people deserve the truth," the king said. "They will get it soon, son, but not yet, not until after I have spoken with my knights, and we have a plan to extinguish the…" King Jared glanced from side to side, then whispered so the stable boy couldn't hear, "…the worgraiths."

A surge of anger and frustration welled within Aiden. He so desperately wanted to say something but dared not cross his father.

King Jared turned toward the door and walked out without another word.

Samuel lay quietly in a room by himself. Normally, there was no such thing as privacy in an infirmary, with cots neatly lined up in rows facing the center of a large room and a half-dozen floor-to-ceiling windows; but at the personal request of the kingdom's second-in-command, Samuel lay in a private room.

Samuel's ribs and legs were bandaged. "Don't give up hope," Sir James, the chief physician, said to Zachariah. "I think it's a concussion and some bone bruises. If his concussion isn't serious, then he should be free to go home soon."

Sir Zachariah was listening, even though his eyes never left his grandson for a moment.

"He'll probably walk with a limp for a while—maybe needing some crutches at first—but that's *if* he doesn't have a serious concussion." Sir James continued. "*And* I have no idea how long he will be unconscious. He could be in a coma for days, weeks, or months. It could even be years. It could be the rest of his life."

Sir James sighed. "I'm sorry I can't tell you anything more definitive than that. It's a miracle he hasn't broken every bone in his body—and that he's even alive."

He put away the remaining bandages and finished wiping the blood off of Samuel's scuff marks. "You say he fell off his dragon? It's not uncommon. Of course, you know that." Sir James took his things and walked toward the door. "I wonder what must have spooked that dragon?"

Zachariah kept his gaze on Samuel. "Thank you." Not hearing a reply, he looked up. Zachariah realized he had been staring at Samuel, lost in thought for a while, and he wondered how long Sir James had been gone.

Zachariah kneeled. "Lord, God, I lost my only son David to a worgraith. Please, I don't know what's going on. It was bad enough Samuel had to face the same creature, the same horrendous situation. Please, heal him fully. Let him wake up—let there be nothing wrong—let him wake up…He is all I have left."

Zachariah wheezed as he breathed deeply, his long hair and beard disheveled. His face was a smudgy mess from wiping so many tears. He bowed so low that his forehead touched the cold marble floor, his sentences scattered.

"Lord, why? Why? You promised there would be pain in this life. But I thought it would never come to this. Don't let me lose my only grandson, Lord. I've lost my wife, I've lost my only son—God, oh Lord—I pray for Franklin and his wife, God, I pray for them."

Zachariah's tired mind blanked for a moment. His thoughts swirled back to Samuel again. "Is there hope for Samuel, Lord?"

And a still, small voice quietly and assuredly said, "Yes."

"Can I have an answer? An answer to why this has happened to me again?" Zachariah continued.

The still, small voice did not answer, but a wash of comfort blanketed Zachariah. He felt a nudge to his spirit: there was something the Lord needed him to do.

"Lord, what must I do? How can I pray?"

"Just wait, and you will see," an inner voice clearly answered.

Then Zachariah felt the stir in his spirit even more. "But what, Lord? What would You have me do?"

"Wait. Wait for my command."

And another wash of comfort swept over Zachariah. He felt a release. His eyes opened, and he felt as if he needn't pray anymore. He stood and made his way back to his chair near Samuel's bed.

"A part, a duty—at my age?" Zachariah asked himself as he pulled the chair closer to the bed.

"What have You left for me to do, oh Lord?"

Still inside the royal stables, Aiden paced like a lion. He looked around to make sure no one was watching or listening. The stable boy had left. Good. Now he was alone with the commonlears.

"God, where are You? What's going on? Do You even exist?" he said in a hushed roar. "If You do, and You can hear me, then let me tell You something. You've killed my mother, You've killed Aeric, and You may have just killed Samuel! My mother and my two best friends!"

Aiden didn't bother looking anymore. He didn't care who was around. "Aren't You a loving God? Aren't You all-powerful, all-seeing, all-knowing? There's so much that's wrong with the world. Maybe You're just useless! Maybe You're lazy, uncaring, or stupid!"

Aiden's voice grew louder as his pacing intensified. "Maybe You really just don't know what's going on down here. Maybe You really can't pay attention to everything that's going on in the world. Maybe these followers of Yours are blindly worshiping something that they think is one thing, but You're really just another."

Aiden threw his riding gloves against the wall and kicked up a cloud of dirt and hay. *They're caught in some mystical hope that doesn't exist. They're just filled with stupid, wishful thinking.*

He turned his head up to the sky and spoke again out loud. "You really don't answer prayers. If You did, then my mother wouldn't have died. You probably don't even know I exist, and it's probably useless for me to waste my breath talking to You because You can't hear me."

Aiden started pacing again. A knot in his stomach grew as his chest tightened. "One thing my mother taught me was that just because you're sitting on a throne doesn't mean you should remain sheltered away, ignorant of the needs of the people. But that's not the way You are."

Aiden clenched his teeth. He noticed he had gotten the attention of some dragons. He turned his head to the floor and spoke more quietly as he walked down the aisle to the doorway. "If You're there, if You're really there—and You really care—if You can hear me and can do something about it, then show me! Prove to me that You care! Show me that You exist!"

As Aiden swung open the stable doors, he noticed something he had witnessed only in drills. At the top of a small tower, a royal guard sounded a large brass bell—the call for all knights within its sound to assemble at once.

As one, the royal messengers mounted the fleet of royal estoy dragons, a breed slightly larger than commonlears with a soft velvet coat of dark lavender fur, and took to the sky. Aiden knew that, as rehearsed in drills many times before, they were carrying a royal decree to the lords and dukes of Whiterock summoning the nobles to the castle with as many knights as they could spare as soon as possible.

Hundreds of estoys leaped from the other set of stables on the opposite side of the castle. He watched as they quickly turned to dots in the air. Aiden's attention turned to the circular building straight ahead—the castle's recovery center. As he strode there, he thought to himself, *Yes, even if it were a drill, it's possible I could have now been one of them—one of the knights—answering the call to duty. But I am not.*

Aiden threw open the doors to the recovery center with a hard shove that let out the last of his emotions. He rushed up the spiral marble staircase. Aiden heard two familiar voices speaking. One was Zachariah, and the other was Sir Brendan of Millbrook. Though Sir Brendan was just barely old enough to be Aiden's father, he seemed more like a big brother. The two men were the knights under whom the three blood brothers had trained.

Aiden tried to hush his footsteps from echoing as his heart pounded.

He neared the room—the same room where his mother had died.

He knocked softly.

"Aiden," Zachariah said in a welcoming tone, "come in. How are you?"

"I'm fine," he lied. "I just came to see how Samuel was doing. He looks…he's all cleaned up and bandaged."

"Yes," Zachariah said. "We don't know if he may have a concussion or how long he might be unconscious. Hope and pray that it's not serious. That's all we can do now."

Aiden felt some tension lift.

"Prayer is an amazing thing," Sir Brendan said. "My father used to say that prayers are the bellows God uses to forge His miracles."

Aiden hid a cringe.

"I can't tell you how many times I've seen prayer work."

Aiden didn't hide his cringe this time, but apparently, no one noticed.

"There are many times when God came through, and I just…" Sir Brendan shook his head. "I just couldn't explain it any other way."

The room was silent for a moment. Aiden just wanted to scream. *Why is it that others can testify to prayer, but I can't?* Aiden took a deep breath. *Perhaps they all attribute a miracle to what is just good luck.* Aiden relaxed. *That must be it.* "Sir Brendan, why aren't you answering the call?"

"The call went out the moment I walked in the door," he said. "I couldn't leave. I had to see how my squire was doing."

Aiden recalled the many times Sir Brendan had apologized for not being able to see them at the test. But the boys understood he had to manage market day security.

"It's amazing, isn't it?" Sir Brendan interrupted Aiden's thoughts. "Worgraiths in Whiterock again?" A gleam in Sir Brendan's eye broke his solemn countenance. He turned to Aiden. "Will you be joining us at the meeting tonight?"

"No. I can't. I'm not a knight."

"But I thought…under the circumstances…"

Neither Zachariah nor Aiden answered. Instead, Aiden sat down in another nearby chair. With eyes on Samuel, he asked the two noblemen, "So, do you want to know exactly what happened this morning?"

Aiden had told them that, if only Aeric had just a moment longer, he could have darted away in time, and he'd be sitting here with them right now. He told them how valiantly Samuel had warded off the beast from killing Aiden. And how Aiden wished he had chased that monster up the mountain; but he didn't tell them why he hadn't—that he was too scared—too frozen in place.

"We must seek God," Zachariah said. "This is a grave situation. I pray there is only one." Zachariah stood and stepped toward the door. Sir Brendan and Aiden stood and followed. Zachariah stopped at the door and turned to them.

"Even if there is only one, how did it get here? The only known worgraiths remaining in the world were last seen far away in the great canyons of the desert countries. And they were just rumors. Strange. Strange indeed." Zachariah turned slowly to the door. "Good day, my friends."

"Good day," Aiden and Sir Brendan replied.

As Zachariah slowly walked down the corridor to the stairs, Sir Brendan took Aiden aside. They walked to a nearby window that overlooked the castle grounds. They watched more knights arrive. "Aiden, I sincerely hope your father will allow you to join us tonight. I've never told you this, but in all the years I have been a knight, just over twenty years now, I have never seen or heard of an apprentice as skilled as you are."

Aiden looked at his mentor with a quick glance. Aiden smiled for the first time in what seemed like such a long time. He searched for words, but he couldn't.

"No one still considered a squire could have done what you, Aeric, and Samuel did today," Sir Brendan continued. "All three of you have been the best squires I have ever seen—or even heard of in my life. You're much better than I was at your age. You're even better than Sir Philip, and that's saying a lot." Sir Brendan smiled briefly. "As far as I'm concerned, both you and Samuel, and Aeric, for that matter, are knights. I only hope your father sees it, too."

"Thank you…I never knew you—"

"Well, now you do." Sir Brendan gave a warm smile. "And don't forget it, because I won't say it again." He winked.

Aiden nodded and returned the smile.

"I'm going to the castle now, and I'll be there for the rest of the day," Sir Brendan said. "I hope to see you at the meeting tonight. Perhaps I can put in a request to your father for you."

Aiden didn't respond. Sir Brendan turned and walked down the hall without another word. Aiden turned and walked back to take another look at Samuel.

"Samuel…please, pull through for me."

It didn't take long for the sight and sound of commonlears to fill the sky.

The villagers stepped out, shielding their eyes from the sun and pointing skyward. The children tried to count them all. Those who were still at the market shouting their wares and entertaining the public halted their shows as their audience seemed more interested in what was going on overhead. Children ran along, trying to keep up with the fast-flying shadows. Parents rounded up their children. They could tell that something was happening. But what?

The shops closed as marketers and entertainers packed up their things to leave town before dusk settled. Market Day was over. This was their cue. Something was happening. And it might be best that the townspeople get home and take shelter. Just in case.

But before everyone could leave, a young man in a royal blue tunic and a matching velvet hat ran onto a platform in the town's square, huffing. Anxiously, he yelled as best as he could above the commotion, "Hear ye, hear ye, citizens of Whiterock, from the village at Whiterock and beyond! Let it be known that the king demands the full attention of all of his people!"

Royal messengers began posting signs all over. Everyone who was trying to head out of the village quickly turned and ran towards the center of town. The people quieted, and those who didn't were hushed by others around them.

"What is it? What is going on?" A husky man from the crowd huffed.

The crier bellowed, "The king demands that everyone take heed, for tomorrow the king's most noble men will ride to the great Whiterock gorge on a most hideous and dire mission. There they will begin slaying dragons."

The crowd gasped as some commotion began among them. "That's no big deal," the husky man said. "There be dragons in every country."

The crier bent down to the man. "Not like these," he said. Then, with a shout, he continued to address the packed audience.

"Worgraiths are back!" he yelled. "I tell you, the Worgraiths are back!"

With worry in their voices and anxiety in their steps, a large commotion began as the crowd quickly dispersed in all directions. Even the husky man turned with panic, shoving those around him, running as fast as he could.

"Go to your homes!" The crier tried to yell above the noise and confusion. "Stay there and do not come out until it is safe!" The noise increased. As the crier continued at the top of his lungs, he could hardly hear himself speak. "The king's men will leave at sunrise, but not without a flyover above the village. You will have your chance to wish them well. Please do so!"

By sunset, nearly six thousand soldiers plus their commonlears, their squires, and lords over the land of Whiterock flooded the island on which Whiterock Palace stood, filling the grassy clearing behind the castle with the sounds of hammers and grunts from a team of squires and pages setting up the encampments. The palace swarmed with well-dressed men in layers of cotton, leather, velvet, and color.

Aiden never liked anyone to feel sorry for him. And he especially didn't want that kind of attention from everyone swarming around now. *Okay, shuffle in quietly, look down, and don't make eye contact. That's it,* Aiden said to himself.

It didn't take long, and without attracting too much attention, Aiden had followed the lords and the commanding knights into one of the castle's manor-like buildings—a lavish lounge larger than one of Whiterock's average-sized homes.

As Aiden weaved around Whiterock's greatest men, the clamor of their talking and bellowing of their laughter was unnerving. He certainly couldn't engage in any conversation if he wanted to—he couldn't brag about how well his squire was coming along, and he couldn't complain about how hard it is to find good help these days. And though he had lived in the castle his whole life, he couldn't comment on the craftsmanship of the room's carved wood paneling or what variety of wood the large beams that stretched just across the ceiling were.

Instead, Aiden just felt the stares. How many would know him by sight, anyway? He certainly didn't recognize them all. He squeezed his way across the plush red carpet and through the rows of chairs that faced the podium.

Aiden peeked through the heads to the enormous stone fireplace. His father was not there. He turned to look at the podium from which his father would speak. Not there, either. Behind the podium was a large window that overlooked a stately courtyard. He didn't seem to be among the knights in the courtyard, either.

"Prince Aiden, so good to see you!"

Aiden almost visibly winced. It was Lord Donovan. Aside from Zachariah, Lord Donovan was the kingdom's highest nobleman. Aiden turned and forced a smile. Lord Donovan, wearing layers of black accented by gold embroidery adorning the contours of his velvet uniform, smiled widely.

"Good to see you, lad." Donovan planted a firm hand on Aiden's shoulder. "I'm sorry to hear about your friend today. It must have been horrible. How are you?"

Aiden answered with only, "Fine. Sad, but fine."

A hush enveloped the room as the soldiers suddenly kneeled, all facing toward the hallway. King Jared had entered the room. Lord Donovan turned to face the king, and both he and Prince Aiden bowed.

"You may rise," King Jared said. "Let us begin. Please, take your seats." Without a word, the noblemen found seats as the king started toward the podium in front of the large glass window that overlooked the outer terrace. But as he began, the king caught Aiden's eye. He called his son forward with the wave of his hand.

"Son, I know why you're here," the king whispered.

"Father, I…"

"Don't interrupt—I am your father, and I am your king. Listen and remain silent." King Jared slightly softened his tone. "The laws of this kingdom require that you should not even be in this room. This meeting is for the highest of nobility and the highest-ranking knights. As for you," King Jared looked around. "I have the authority to make exceptions to certain rules. I'll allow you to at least attend this meeting. But don't think that because I am letting you here, because you are the son of a king, and because of your bravery this morning, you have the right, the privilege, or the permission to partake in this mission."

Aiden felt a sense of fatherly fear that he hadn't felt in a long time.

King Jared sighed deeply. His face sagged with burden. Aiden noticed for the first time how hard it was for his father to balance being a parent and a king. In an almost regretful tone, King Jared spoke more mildly to his son. "You may have survived. You may have proven yourself heroic, but you are not yet a knight, and certainly not one of the highest ranked knights in the kingdom."

"Yes, sir," Aiden whispered. "I understand."

Without another word, the king turned, and Aiden searched for a place to sit. Aiden could plainly see that all the chairs were taken. So, he stood out of the way and off to the side like he originally intended, near where Sir Brendan and Sir Zachariah were sitting. He caught their glances as he passed by. Aiden sensed they shared his father's take on the subject. Or perhaps it was the look on his own face that told them.

Making no ceremony or introduction, King Jared began speaking. "Gentlemen of our kingdom, most trusted lords and knights, we have a situation that I hoped would never happen again in our territory. There are no better words, nor apparently any reason, to deliver my speech with any sort of eloquence. Gentlemen, I can only speak plainly—there are worgraiths in Whiterock again."

Voices erupted in the room. Some uttered concern while others expressed their eagerness to get the job done. Only a few said nothing.

King Jared raised his hand to control the noise. "Gentlemen, Gentlemen." The room hushed, and the king paused for a moment, his reddened eyes watered.

"One of our bravest squires, Aeric of the Green—Sir Franklin's only son—died at the hands of one of the dreaded monsters this morning. My son and Zachariah's grandson, Samuel of the Moorland, were with him. Samuel is safe and in the recovery center. We pray for his quick improvement. My son escaped harm, and as you may already know, is with us at this meeting." King Jared eyed Aiden. Then, he looked down at his podium, and gripped it tightly with both hands, searching for words as the men applauded.

Aiden didn't know what to do. Now everyone was staring at him—and applauding. For what?

The king loosened his grasp on the podium and gazed around the room and into the eyes of his men as the applause died down. "Just three courageous squires fought this beast. Though it survives, this is a remarkable feat as you are all well aware—some of you too well aware—considering it sometimes requires a squadron of men to kill just one worgraith. I publicly commend the bravery and skill of not just my son," he looked back at Aiden, "but also his companions for their skillful fighting, especially considering the size, strength, and speed of these creatures."

Now all the noblemen stood. They faced Aiden and applauded. He heard cheers and undistinguished shouts of approval.

I do not deserve this.

The sea of men standing, looking at him, and applauding blocked his view of his father. Aiden glanced at Sir Brendan and Zachariah, who both held the largest smiles of anyone in the room. Aiden returned their beaming smiles with an awkward smile of his own.

As the group sat, Aiden and his father locked eyes. Tears streamed down the king's face, and Aiden had never seen such a proud expression on anyone before. What a contrast from just a few moments ago. His father beamed at him, proud, exalting him in public. The kingdom's most highly respected men hailed him a hero.

If only Samuel and Aeric were here to receive this honor as well. They truly deserve it.

The room quieted. The knights seemed to have gathered a bit of a spark after having heard the story of the brave young men.

After a brief pause, the king spoke. "We do not know how many worgraiths are in the kingdom. I pray the task will not require all of us, but worgraiths travel in packs. It's highly unlikely that there was just one. There could be anywhere from a half dozen to a dozen who have already made their lairs within the caves of the gorge. We need to expedite our mission and hunt down these worgraiths as quickly as possible so that these monsters do not find their way to this palace and this city, spreading death and destruction across this kingdom and inflicting devastation everywhere."

A few shouted in approval.

"As you know, these creatures simply hunt and breed. That is it. Unlike most dragons, they have no care for anyone or anything. They care not about treasure troves or magic, nor do they wish to communicate or make war or peace. We cannot tame worgraiths like our commonlears, condolears, or estoys. Worgraiths breed, and they hunt. Except for their own kind, everything that moves is their prey."

The king's voice softened. He placed his hands together in a praying gesture and pressed his forefingers against his mouth as he paced. "Tonight, those of us in this room shall share a meal together, and then we will awaken at dawn's first light. In these autumn days, light is precious; we must take advantage of every moment. If a second expedition is required the following morning, we will camp in the gorge until we find and destroy all the worgraiths."

The king's speech received a rousing round of applause and shouts of cheer. He raised his hand to quiet the crowd. "It has always been my pleasure to appoint Sir Zachariah as my steward when I am away from my throne. However, due to the health of his grandson, my old friend has respectfully declined. I have extended this invitation, therefore, to Sir Donovan of the Glen."

There was an eruption of applause. Except from Aiden.

"As you can certainly guess, if you don't know already, Sir Donovan's manor, and much of his land, is near to where we will be fighting. Therefore, by appointing him to remain here, I am keeping him from defending his own land. This is not a slight to the lord by any means, but that I trust you and am privileged to have him serve in this capacity while I am away."

There was another resounding applause. Lord Donovan stood, and King Jared gestured his hand toward Sir Donovan, allowing him to speak.

"Thank you, King Jared, for this opportunity to serve you in this capacity," Lord Donovan said as the applause diminished. "I am humbled at your request and am honored to serve as your steward."

"Thank you," King Jared replied.

"King, fellow noblemen, and soldiers," Lord Donovan continued. "For those who have not yet had the privilege, it is my pleasure to introduce you to my son, who achieved knighthood a year ago. He is my heir and will therefore serve as one among the many worthy defenders of my land and manor during this mission while I am here. I present to you Sir Philip of the Glen."

The crowd applauded as Sir Philip stood.

Ugh, I never understood why Alicia was so enamored with that spoiled louse.

As Philip sat, Lord Donovan continued,

"King, now that your son is a knight, will the two of you be on this expedition together? I think it would be wonderful to see a father-son mission take place."

As Sir Brendan and Zachariah looked at Aiden with surprise, the crowd's favor grew, eventually swelling into a loud cheer.

King Jared looked around. "My son and Samuel are not knights," he tried to interject above the applause. "They did not finish the test."

King Jared paused and looked down at the podium. As the applause died down, his words came slowly. "It seems I must confess, though, that the young men's bravery, which I had acknowledged tearfully just moments ago, makes my son worthy of being a knight. He had not the chance to finish the test, but…joining us on this expedition seems to be…appropriate, regardless of the official rules of the test."

A quick burst of applause interrupted the king's speech again. The king looked directly at his son. "As much as it pains me for this particular expedition to be my son's first, I must come to terms with what I already had conceded in my heart—that Aiden did remarkably more than what the test had required—certainly earning him the right to be a knight." The king took a breath. "Aiden…will you join us on this quest?"

All eyes turned to Aiden. His heart pounded. His breathing stopped. Prince Aiden quietly replied, "I will. But I do not wish to be knighted without Samuel—if he should recover."

King Jared nodded slowly and smiled. "So it shall be. We will wait for Samuel to recover before the official knighting ceremony."

Cheering erupted again. King Jared raised his hands to quiet the audience. "Men, let us disperse. But not before we seek guidance from the Almighty. Please stand." Everyone stood and bowed their heads. King Jared prayed. "Lord, God, the King of all kings. Humbly, we request Your mercy, grace, and provision. We request Your hand of protection to guide us safely; Your peace to be in our hearts; Your wisdom to rule in our minds; Your strength to give us strength…"

Then the king paused. A look of puzzlement momentarily came across his face. His head cocked slightly, as if he heard something. "And shield us with a greater quantity of Your mighty angels. Amen." As the king left the podium, he began singing a hymn of praise. One voice after another joined in. The room was soon full of praise to the King of Kings. Peace poured out as if overflowing from a reservoir. Although he couldn't deny its presence, Aiden found himself disengaged. Looking across the room, he noticed he was not the only one. Philip seemed almost sickened by this display of worship.

Feeling eyes following him, Aiden quietly slipped out of the room. He did not want to spend the next hour talking with everyone in sight about how it felt to be part of the mission now, about everything that he had gone through that day, and getting incessant congratulations on the success of fighting a worgraith and living to tell about it "at such a young age." Aiden did not want to hear anyone's sympathy for his friends, either.

FOUR

Just before daybreak, Alicia stood alone on a large stone platform that led to the back courtyard. The gusty wind diminished her torchlight enough that she couldn't see who was stirring around the encampments. It didn't help that the dark, marching clouds had concealed the brilliant stars. The full moon peeked out now and again, and when it didn't, it softly glowed through the heavy, fast-moving cover.

Alicia's breath whisked like smoke in the breezy, frosty air. She shivered. With her free hand, she tugged a heavy fur-lined overcoat tightly around her and walked down a few steps onto the grass. She should have worn something warmer than silk slippers. Her toes instantly stung from the quickly accumulating frost that crunched beneath her feet.

For six thousand soldiers, there was barely any sound. A few snuffs and rumbles from dragons awakening, some scrapes of metal against metal, low mumbling voices, and a burst of gruff laughter was all she heard.

Some shadowy movements around the morning's campfires helped her piece together what was she was hearing—a few squires out fetching this and that, making breakfast, and getting commonlears groomed and ready for the hunt.

The campfires unexpectedly took Alicia back in her memory to the memorial luminaries that were lit for her mother not long after she had died.

Alicia had to stand on tiptoes and peer over the rail of her father's balcony. There, cuddled close to her father, she and Aiden watched luminaries light at dusk—one by one, stretching as far as the eye could see, thousands upon thousands of them—from the village at Whiterock to the horizon in every direction, all along the gorge and dotting heavenward up Whiterock mountain. Knights rode softly and graciously in the sky, holding torches in counterpoint to millions of stars. Alicia would never forget that beautiful sight and the love poured out from the villagers and nobility in honor of her mother's memory.

Alicia shivered again as a brief wind swept up. All night long she thought about the mission, the men, her brother, father, and Philip. She had hoped that maybe she could glimpse Philip, get his attention, or fetch a squire to bring him to her. Alicia had to see him; she had to talk to him before preparations got too hectic. Since Philip lived relatively close, he could have stayed in his father's manor for the night instead. Either way, she was going to stay right there in the cold until—

"Alicia!"

The young princess quickly turned to the side and saw the dark outline of a tall young man hastily making his way up the knoll.

"Philip!"

Alicia held back everything within her from running and embracing him—after all, she was nobility. *Act like a lady,* she reminded herself as she hurried to meet him as quickly as she thought proper.

"Philip, I was looking for you," Alicia said as her heart fluttered.

Philip looked as if he had been awake and ready for hours, neatly groomed and well dressed in a black leather tunic and a heavy white padded shirt underneath. He had black velvet pants and knee-high black leather dragon-riding boots. His eyes sparkled back at her as his thin smile widened.

"I looked up and saw you in the distance, so I had to come see you. What are you doing out here at this hour by yourself?"

Alicia looked at the ground. "I came out to see you."

"I'm glad you did, because I have something for you. I wanted to give this to you privately before it got too hectic around here." He reached into a pouch slung around his waist. He pulled out something metallic.

Alicia's heart fluttered. A nervous laugh escaped.

Philip opened his hand. The silver chain sparkled from the light of Alicia's lantern. Dangling from the necklace, framed in gold, was a round red diamond polished to perfection.

"This is for you," he said.

Alicia gasped. "Oh, Philip, I've never seen anything so beautiful. The color is so brilliant…you must have spent a fortune…"

"There is nothing too costly for you, my lady. Here." He placed the necklace around her. "This is so you can keep me near your heart."

Alicia's heart lifted. She held her breath. She wanted to embrace Philip, but she clasped his hand instead. "I will miss you." A solitary tear ran down her cheek. "Come back safe."

Philip whispered, "This may seem sudden, but I cannot keep from asking you this any longer. I do not know how else to say this, but…" Philip bent down on one knee. "Princess, will you marry me? When I return from this mission, I wish to take you as my wife."

Alicia swept her hand from Philip's to cover her mouth, which hardly concealed a brief squeal. She wished he would ask her someday, but she certainly did not expect today, not now.

"Yes. Yes, of course I will. Oh, my father will be so pleased."

"I hope so," Philip said. "I haven't asked him yet for your hand, so please keep this a secret until I return. Then, I will ask him and give you a ring."

"You haven't asked him yet? I…I don't feel right about this. You must ask him. Please."

"I will, when I…"

"No. Now."

"What? Now? I mean, we are about to head out on a mission of great importance. Daylight has not even broken yet. I don't want to…"

"No, please. I'll lead you to him. I know right where he is. He's visiting Samuel before going on the mission."

"Princess, you want me to ask him for your hand while he's visiting Samuel? This isn't the proper time nor place for such…"

"But Philip, it's the only time you'll have before leaving. Ask him. We should do this properly."

Philip followed Alicia to the recovery center. "Hold on. It seems your father might get suspicious if we both entered the room."

"You're right," Alicia said. "But don't leave for the mission without seeing me first."

"Oh, I won't," Philip replied.

King Jared stood over Samuel's infirmary bed. The young squire was still in a deep sleep. "You seem at peace," the king said. "I suppose that's a good sign. Lord, send Your healing touch. You've spared Samuel from the hand of the worgraith. He's come home alive; I pray that You wake him and fully restore him. Please heal him. Please, spare his life. For Zachariah. For Aiden. Let me place my father's sword on his shoulders and dub him a knight, with Aiden by his side. Amen."

King Jared heard a noise at the door. He turned. It was Philip. "Ah, come in."

Lord Donovan looked himself over in a gold-framed mirror that stretched from floor to ceiling. He hardly dressed in any other colors than black with gold embroidery. This time, he only accented his costume with red silk on the underside of his black velvet cape.

A knock came at the door.

"Yes?"

"Your coach is ready, sire. Polished from top to bottom."

Lord Donovan tugged at his gloves once more, and then without another word, he turned from the mirror and walked by his servant without acknowledgment. He strode swiftly out of his manor with head held high.

Like his outfit, the coach was made of ebony and trimmed in gold, with the inside of his carriage lined in red velvet. His hired driver opened the door to the coach, and the lord entered without a word. The four black condolear dragons, similar but a tad larger and stouter than commonlears, raised their wings to prepare for flight. They were adorned in similar colors—black reins with gold studs.

A stately old driver—also dressed in black velvet—cracked a long whip as he chomped on the end of a pipe. The condolears flapped their wings and pulled the carriage forward out of the portico, which functioned as the centerpiece of the manor. With only a few steps, the condolears had no more stone—nor anything else under their feet. Lord Donovan's manor sat on an appendage of the southern end of Whiterock Gorge. The manor extended high above the gorge as a massive arched bridge. The condolears glided smoothly, straight off the end of the architectural wonder, and flew graciously out above the ravine, heading westward to Whiterock Palace.

It was another honor of knighthood that Aiden would have to wait for. Holding back a solitary tear from streaming down his face, he couldn't help but think of Aeric never having this chance he so longed for. The prince donned his fighting gear in the privacy of his own bedroom—a heavy undershirt, chain mail, royal blue cotton arming coat and pants, along with black leg, chest, and forearm leather then leg, foot, arm, and torso armor. He wore a royal red surcoat with a stately gold commonlear dragon on hind legs guarding a crown embroidered on the front, symbolizing the royal coat of arms.

In the stables, he dressed Lucy in her chain mail, leather, and armor. "As much as I have looked forward to this moment, Lucy, I'm scared."

She gave a nod and a snort, telling him she understood.

"I can't believe it. I never thought it would be like this. I looked so forward to it, but now, it's different." He patted Lucy's neck. "I feel so alone without Samuel and Aeric. And I still feel guilty. Why did we survive without a scratch when they…" Aiden sighed deeply and looked around to see that no one was listening.

"I have my father," he added. "And I have Sir Brendan." He took a deep breath and then snapped the last part of her bridle. "There, you're done. Now I think we're ready."

A trumpet sounded outside. "Just in time," Aiden said. "It's our call. Are you ready for this?"

Lucy nodded with a snort and then nuzzled her nose against his face.

"All right, let's do this." Aiden walked Lucy out of the stables. A few others were lingering and finishing tacking up their dragons.

As Aiden and Lucy walked out, they saw the horde of other knights assembled for duty in a clearing near the tents. Aiden's father wore the same battle gear as his knights and noblemen— with the addition of his royal red cape and small gold crown. He stood on the same stone platform on which Alicia had stood just hours ago, moments before her betrothal, with his commonlear at his side, ready to address his men. Zachariah stood with him, and a series of thrones lined the platform.

Aiden's attention on his father ended abruptly as a commonlear bluntly nosed him in the shoulder, nearly knocking him to the ground. It felt purposeful. Looking over to see whose commonlear it was, Aiden found a smirk awaiting him. It was Philip.

"So, you and I are going to be brothers-in-law."

"What?" Aiden asked.

"You haven't heard yet?"

Aiden furrowed his eyebrows. "No, I haven't heard anything; what are you talking about?"

"When I return, I will become a member of the royal family."

"What?"

"I asked your father for your sister's hand in marriage. Surely you know that we've been courting?"

Aiden let out an involuntary, audible moan. Philip's commonlear butted Aiden's shoulder again. Lucy gave an angry snort. "I would watch your attitude if I were you," Philip said as he looked at both Aiden and Lucy. He let out a sinister smile. "Then again, after today…" Philip's grin crept wider. A second trumpet sounded the call to arms, and without another word, Philip turned and walked to meet his group.

As Aiden turned to walk to his unit, he noticed Alicia sitting in one of the small thrones next to their father's on the royal platform. She looked like a young queen. But if Aiden had anything to do with it, she wouldn't be queen or lady with that viper, Philip, by her side.

Aiden could see that her eyes caught Philip's, and she gave him a bright smile. Instead of making his way in line, Aiden approached Alicia.

"Am I to believe that you are engaged to that snake?"

"Aiden!" Alicia said, trying to keep her voice low. "How dare you? Philip is a brave and chivalrous man!"

"Didn't you just see what he did to me?"

"Aiden, why do you hate him so?"

"No, see, he hates me…"

"No, he's told me…"

"What? What has he told you?"

"He doesn't hate you. He wants to be your friend."

"What? Alicia," Aiden took a moment to force himself to lower his voice. "I'm telling you, there is something about that man." Aiden leaned forward. He grit his teeth, eyes burning with anger. "He's conceited, selfish, spoiled, angry…he's only going to hurt you."

Alicia looked away. Her eyes watered slightly. "It looks like Father is about to start. I suggest you get in line."

Aiden could tell he had crossed a line. "I'm only trying to help," he said.

Alicia uttered not a word, letting her face speak instead. Aiden turned and walked to stand among the men. It didn't take long for him to find his unit, as each group lined up behind a nobleman who held high the banner of their shire in the front. Once Aiden found his place among the Whiterock village unit, he looked back at his sister. She certainly was becoming a young lady. It was almost as if he were looking at his mother again.

Aiden's concentration broke when his father took to the podium. "Gentlemen of the kingdom, as you know, it has been sixteen years since Whiterock gathered together the force of men I see before me—nearly six thousand knights, not including all of your squires."

The king looked over his men, dressed in shining armor. "And it is for the same unfortunate circumstance we meet again. Not long from now, we will take to Whiterock Gorge to slay these worgraiths so that they may not come to us and lay waste our lands as they tried to do not long ago. We pray that God's favor will rest upon us—I know it will."

As the king spoke those words, a whooshing sound reverberated from above. It was Lord Donovan arriving in his coach.

King Jared did not seem displeased by this interruption. Instead, as if he were expecting it to be timed just so, the coach descended and landed near the podium. Lord Donovan's condolears then drove the coach to the side of the platform where a servant walked out and opened the door. Lord Donovan stepped out and then bowed before the king. The king nodded in acceptance, gesturing for the lord to come forward. Lord Donovan approached the podium.

Many knights in Sir Philip's unit proudly watched their lord take the podium, but Sir Philip's gaze was on Alicia, who tried to hide her smile as she looked back at him. She couldn't. Sir Philip tried hard as well, but he, too, could not hold a smile back.

Aiden's eyes remained at the podium as Lord Donovan kneeled before King Jared. A sudden hatred for Lord Donovan arose within Aiden at this moment. There was no specific reason to hate him. He was Philip's father. That was enough.

King Jared placed his sword on the lord's shoulders. "With the witnesses before me and by God Almighty, I hereby place all matters of state in your hands until I return. Rise Lord Donovan, Steward of Whiterock."

As Lord Donovan rose, the men bowed to him. Aiden was the last to bow, and he did not fully kneel or bow his head.

"You may rise," King Jared said. As the men rose, Lord Donovan took his place on the line of thrones. King Jared resumed, "Gentlemen, let us ask for divine guidance and strength on this most grievous task." King Jared lifted his hands, closed his eyes, and tilted his head Heavenward. "Lord, we honor you this day. We ask Your hand of protection upon us as we fight to rid this kingdom of worgraiths—once and for all. This is not our battle, but Yours. We place it in Your hands. Grant us Your favor. Grant us triumph for the sake of the people of Whiterock. Amen."

The knights shouted *amen*. Without a word, King Jared stepped from the podium.

The knights went back to examining their commonlears again. Some doled out discipline to their squires for their minor shortcomings—the belts were too tight or not tight enough, the arrows were on the wrong side again, and so on. Other knights petted and tried to calm their worried dragon companions and gave a few encouraging words to them. Some knights handed written messages to their squires that they wish to be read to their families in the event something might happen.

With determination in each step, Philip walked briskly and confidently to see Alicia. They couldn't take their eyes off each other. Once he reached a short distance from the stage, Philip stopped to look at his father and addressed him first.

"Father," he said.

"Son," Donovan said, sauntering toward him on the platform, hands outstretched. "I am so proud of you."

"I am proud of you, too, father, and I must say, having you on the kingdom's throne seems, well, fitting."

King Jared walked up. "Is your son telling you about the conversation we had this morning, Lord Donovan?"

"No," the lord replied.

"Well," King Jared said, deciding to take the lead. "Your son will soon become royalty."

"What?" a surprised Donovan exclaimed, turning to his son.

"Alicia and I are betrothed."

"Oh, that's great news. Great news indeed!"

King Jared chuckled warmly. "He will make a great addition to our family."

"He certainly will," Lord Donovan said. "He certainly will. Oh, I am so happy for the both of you. May I?" the lord asked King Jared as his arms stretched outward toward Alicia. The king gave an approving nod, allowing Philip's father an opportunity to embrace her.

"Oh," Donovan said, "you will be like the daughter I never had. It is a shame that we never had another child." Donovan's expression dimmed. "My wife, Karyssa, died in childbirth, as you know. Philip luckily survived. I had to raise him all on my own, and of course, I hardly had time for him. His nanny, too, God rest her soul, died when Philip was eleven." Lord Donovan shook his head slowly. "From then on, he practically raised himself, except for his knight, who taught him everything he knew about knighthood and chivalry." Donovan looked at his son. "Now, my Philip is a man. And he turned out more wonderfully than I could have ever imagined."

At that, King Jared heartily agreed and let the father and son say their goodbyes privately. The king walked over to his daughter and gave her the biggest hug she ever had in her life. He looked her in the eyes, sighed, and said, "I will return. I promise."

Eyes welling with tears, Alicia hugged her father as tightly as she had when she was a child, her head snuggled firmly on his shoulder.

The king sighed as he looked at his daughter one more time. "Oh, how you have grown. You've turned into a beautiful reflection of your mother." The king turned and looked at Lord Donovan. "I know I am leaving the kingdom in expert hands until I return."

"Thank you. It is my honor. May the Almighty be with you," the kingdom's steward said.

King Jared looked at Philip, then Alicia. Then he turned and walked off the stage to his soon-to-be son-in-law, put his hand on his shoulder and said, "I'm proud to call you son."

King Jared looked over his shoulder at a beaming Lord Donovan, and then, without a word, the king walked down from the platform and over to his dragon, which faced his men.

Aiden was checking over his gear and making sure the straps and buckles were tight on Lucy when he peered over his shoulder and saw his father approach.

Looking further behind him, he saw Philip was now walking toward his dragon, and Alicia was looking directly at Aiden. As she smiled at him, something in her expression told him she was proud of her brother. Aiden smiled back and realized they had forgiven each other. Not that all was settled, but he'd have to find a way to deal with Philip when he got back. First things first. Aiden mounted Lucy, face like flint. While he watched the squadrons group themselves together, a voice broke his concentration.

"Good luck, Aiden. I'm proud."

Aiden looked over his other shoulder. It was Sir Brendan. A comforting face set his heart and mind at ease. "Glad to see you," Aiden replied.

"I mean that," Sir Brendan said. "I really am proud. I want you to know that there are others here as well who may not say so but agree that it is good to see you on this expedition. You've certainly earned the right to be among these men."

"Thank you," Aiden said.

"Ready men?" the king bellowed. After the troops gave their king a hearty affirmative shout, he snapped his commonlear's reins and shouted, "For Whiterock!"

"For Whiterock!" The army shouted and raised their swords. Enoch flapped his wings and slowly ascended, giving the king's men the cue to rise. As they swiftly ascended, shouts of encouragement and adoration erupted from the squires, accompanied by enthusiastic applause from Alicia, Zachariah, and Lord Donovan on the stone platform. The brave soldiers ascended several hundred feet, and then, in parade-like formation, headed toward the village at Whiterock.

Aiden glanced around him and saw six thousand men on six thousand colorful commonlears, each in bright, shining armor, filling the sky with the splendid insignias of their kingdom and their lord's manor. If it was an awesome sight from Aiden's perspective, it must have been brilliant from the ground.

"If only Samuel could be here," Aiden muttered under his breath, almost in tears. "Aeric." Aiden shook his head. "How I miss Aeric right now."

The knights flew low over the village at Whiterock. King Jared allowed two men to fly just behind him, one on each side, each bearing the flag of Whiterock—a royal red flag with a gold commonlear dragon on hind legs guarding the crown. Each man leading his lord's shire waived their shire's flag as well.

Within a short amount of time, the citizens who had not fled to the countryside had decked out their city in honor of the courageous soldiers going off to slay the monstrous dragons. By now, the villagers' worry had turned to hope. Townspeople threw streamers from second and third-story windows; banners stretched from rooftop to rooftop; children—some sitting on their daddy's shoulders—waved small flags while adults waved large ones. Those who did not have flags brandished kerchiefs instead.

Musicians sounded their trumpets to hail the incoming heroes. Throughout the city, several thousand people of every age looked skyward, shouting, hopping, and waving their hands. They cheered the glorious parade of heroes colorfully soaring low against the backdrop of an ominously darkening sky.

The kingdom's bravest men sailed over the city twice, nearly scraping the rooftops, in a spiral formation, allowing the citizens an opportunity to wish their men farewell and good luck. The king waved his hand to greet his people during the last pass and then led his men out to battle.

FIVE

The mass of soldiers soon made their way to the edge of Whiterock Gorge. By the time the king's squadron passed the first waterfall at the crescent break, King Jared had requested his son to fly close to him.

"Where were you just before it happened?"

"It was between here and the bend. He must have come from up there." Aiden pointed to jagged rocks along the opposite cliff. "In that direction."

King Jared signaled the squadrons to stop and hover where they were. He reached into a sack behind his saddle and pulled out a long, thin, red telescope.

"It must have perched in that crevice." King Jared put the telescope to his eye. "It would be a perfect hideout for a worgraith." The king took a moment to carefully examine the crevice then scanned the area further. "I don't see anything. But we'll remain cautious. You never know where or when one might blast out from nowhere." The king put the telescope back in the pouch. "The best thing to do is to fly above the canyon and spot below," he told his son. "Usually, worgraiths like to fly within the shade and concealment of the gorge; and flying above gives us more time to see one coming."

Aiden looked back at his father's army, lined up like bait. Philip's team was keeping watch from the rear. *Thank God we're nowhere near each other,* Aiden thought.

As the army continued to press forward to Whiterock Mountain, Aiden glanced over at his father. The expression on the king's face revealed nothing but determination. Aiden noticed there was no sound except for the almost tranquilizing flapping of thousands of commonlear wings.

In a short time, and with no sign of worgraiths, the king had led his troops safely to the top of Whiterock Mountain. The summit was always spectacular. Only pure white marble surrounded them. The places where the stone was quarried to build Whiterock Palace had created man-made rock cliffs that seemed like an arena of giant steps. In some places, the carved stone seemed like its own mini gorge. And because there was nothing else immediately surrounding them, other places along the white marbled top seemed as if they were in a whole other world. It was from here that the army could view the entire canyon weaving through the valley. Even though the leaves had fallen, making it easier to see into the ravine, it was impossible to see the entire forest floor.

King Jared furrowed his brow, heaved a sigh, and gave his men permission to take a quick break. The flag bearers put away their flags, and the soldiers gave their dragons a brief snack and drink from a canteen. But it seemed the men and their steeds were a bit too on edge and eager to put this mission to rest.

King Jared peered again with his telescope. "I don't see anything," he said softly to Sir Brendan. "I had hoped that we could have seen at least one stirring somewhere and ambushed it from above, but…" King Jared put his telescope down, sighed again, and said somberly, "Spread the news. We are going in."

Not long after the kingdom's bravest men had flown off to war, the bustle of the joyous sendoff had quieted down. A somber hush fell over the village and castle grounds.

Princess Alicia had walked slowly up the staircase into her cool, quiet bedroom, nestled in a tower that faced Whiterock Gorge. With her father, brother and now-fiancé gone, her learning activities cancelled, and her lady-in-waiting absent, a stark lonliness enveloped her. She walked out onto her balcony and peered across her father's kingdom. She looked across the gorge to Whiterock Mountain. There was no sight or sound of conflict, just a quiet breeze. Though she took that as a sign they were alright, a knot twisted in her stomach, and her chest tightened. She held a breath and tried to let it out slowly.

As the breeze settled, she drank in some short-lived warmth brought by the autumn sun as it peeked from behind a dense cloud. Breathing in the sweet air that accompanied this time of year, Alicia closed her eyes and said a quiet prayer. "Lord, please be with the men on their mission. Lead them, Lord, safely. Let this be quick and simple. Don't let a single man fall in battle. *Please*, let them *all* return safely."

Amid the uncertainty of what was to come, she felt a sudden peace. Her heart skipped as her thoughts turned to Philip. "Lord, guide him, direct—"

A deep uneasiness twisted her heart.

"Lord? Direct him, guide him—" There it was again, harder, more discerning.

"What, Lord? Are you telling me something?"

A still, small voice whispered in her spirit. But she couldn't quite understand what it was trying to tell her. It was as if the spirit was whispering too softly. It was as if her worry for the safety of the men was blocking it, but she had the distinct impression the still, small voice whispered something like, "No. This is wrong."

"Is it something about Philip? Is he going to die? Wait…" She sensed something more. "Aiden and Philip? What about Aiden and Philip?"

Then the presence in her spirit aligned with her thoughts of Aiden and Philip, twisted her heart, and sunk it.

"Lord, tell me, what is wrong? What are you saying? What about Philip? What about Aiden?"

The spirit didn't respond, leaving her heart still twisted like wet clay.

"Lord, I'm confused. What does this mean, exactly? Did I hear wrong? Is this just my imagination?" She paused, thought about it some more, and then said aloud, "That must be it, just my imagination. I'm just too worried about this mission…"

Then, like a falling star bursting through a clear, dark night, Alicia remembered Samuel. Yes, it seemed like the perfect time to visit him.

The canyon was completely still. Only the burbling of Spring Creek reverberated off the canyon walls.

The king commanded his men to split up into three groups. King Jared led the first group; Sir Graehme led the second; and Sir Slade led the third. Each took flight to canvass the gorge—King Jared at the eastern end, Sir Graehme at the western; and Sir Slade's group covered a smaller southern gorge that branched out from Whiterock Mountain—the gorge where Lord Donovan's manor was located. This fulfilled King Jared's promise to Lord Donovan: Lord Donovan's own knights would protect his land.

Tall, broad, and handsome with thick, blond hair and misty blue eyes, Sir Slade was the highest-ranking of Lord Donovan's knights still able to perform in battle. He trained Sir Philip and was among the most highly respected men in the kingdom. He had been there the night before, in the castle lounge with Philip, when Aiden was asked to join the fight.

King Jared felt remorseful for having assigned Sir Slade this task, though. There had been no sign of worgraiths in the smaller canyon. Surely, if there were, the lord and his men would not only have known and reported it by now, but with their reputation, would have already conquered at least one.

The stream was swift and deep where King Jared's regiment had landed—on an upper ledge near where Aeric had died. It was where the stone walking trail ended. King Jared's ancestors had commissioned the pathways, a system of natural walkways, stone steps, and ornate bridges that led through the gorge.

From there, King Jared took out his telescope once again and surveyed as much as he could. He gave a hefty sigh and put away his telescope. "Men, I'm sure most of you have come to this conclusion already," he said. "We must lure the worgraiths out of hiding. We've got to go through the canyon and let them find us. That means we will be bait for them, but there is no other way. Say your prayers."

Alicia held back a tear as she looked upon the unconscious Samuel. This was the first time she had seen anyone in the infirmary since her mother died. Alicia sat down at Samuel's bedside, held his hand, and said a prayer. As she began in nearly silent whispers, her head bowed and eyes closed, she sensed a movement on the pillow and heard a faint mumble.

With eyes barely open, he turned his head to her.

"Hello." Alicia smiled. This time, she did not suppress a tear. She squeezed his hand. Her heart beat faster.

"Where am I?" he murmured.

"You're in the infirmary—at the castle. How are you?"

"I…I'm dizzy…and you're blurry." Samuel flinched as he adjusted himself. "Ow!"

"What's wrong?" Alicia asked.

"Oh," Samuel whispered, "my head is pounding, and my legs feel like they're bent all out of shape. My ribs are sore…"

"The physicians and nurses don't think you've broken anything, at least that they can see—"

"If I don't have any broken bones," Samuel rasped, "that means I can get out of here, right?"

"Well," she said, "I think you'll need some time. But you can probably leave fairly soon, I'd think."

"I feel like vomiting."

"Oh! I'll get a nurse."

Sir Graehme's knights flew back to the canyon entrance. A horrid screech broke the silence just above them. They turned with a jolt.

A black worgraith hunched on a ledge with its wings out, ready to strike. The worgraith had already sprung out in full force by the time Sir Graehme came to his senses.

"Split up!" he yelled. "Then flank the thing! Attack it with everything you've got!" As the words escaped his lips, the commonlears darted in fright. He nearly lost control of his own dragon, which almost flung him in a fearful escape.

In an instant, the worgraith had snatched several men and their dragons in each hand.

Fire spewed from the dragon's mouth. The soldiers did all they could to combat the beast while scrambling to remove themselves from the fury of its flames. But the eruption consumed nearly a quarter of Sir Graehme's men in one fell swoop.

But the quickness of the commonlears and the steadfast commitment of the remaining soldiers soon turned their fear into fight. They did as their leader commanded and flanked the monster on every side, peppering it with arrows.

The giant dragon flinched, winced, and roared. It lifted its arms in defense. In pain, the monster clenched its jaw and clamped its fists, squeezing its freshly caught meal tightly in each hand and mangling the dead bodies into one big glop.

Roaring with fury, the giant beast threw the bloody mess to the ground. Its eyes burned with hatred and anger. Brow furrowed, the worgraith clenched its teeth as a low growl followed by a greater, more frightening roar erupted from its throat. Fire fumed from its mouth again, dropping its enemies like scorched stones all along the canyon as it endured the attack on every side.

The monster swatted the adversaries all around it, but its might and power were not enough to keep all the soldiers at bay. The king's men were determined to win.

Sir Graehme gathered several of his men to swarm the beast's face. They shot at it and gouged out its eyes, which caused it to flail its head and jerk its body backwards. The monster lost its balance. As it blindly tumbled, it thrashed its arms and mighty tail in vengeance behind him, hoping to smash as many adversaries as possible.

Knights flew off their commonlears. Others outside the maelstrom of the worgraith's resistance bravely continued to fight against the beast, assailing it with everything they had. The commonlears then joined—ripping, tearing, biting, and clawing at the beast.

The great black worgraith rose to its feet, determined to kill, determined to win. Swinging its arms wherever it sensed riders zooming past, it cast fire in every direction, destroying a quarter more.

"Retreat!" Sir Graehme ordered. "Retreat!"

A trumpet sounded the call to draw back. Some did, but a large group of men stayed, determined to win or die trying.

Sir Graehme and several of his men watched from safety as these diligent warriors suffered the vengeance of the worgraith. Veteran and novice alike ignored the calls to withdraw. They died at the hands of the beast—all of them—all the ones who stayed and fought.

Sir Graehme lost more than half of his men on that charge alone. The monster, although victorious, was now blinded. Though it had a feast waiting for it, it could not find the food it had fought for.

It dropped to its knees. The men, though injured, observed safely from a distance. The worgraith sunk its shoulders low and let out a mournful wail that turned into a hate-filled cry.

"What do we do now, sir?" one survivor asked Sir Graehme, unable to control the shaking in his voice.

"I don't know," he replied. "This worgraith is not as I remember them to be."

"Aiden went?" Samuel asked with a weak smile. Every bone in his body moaned. "Alongside all the kingdom's knights?"

"Yes," Alicia said. Worry filled her eyes.

Samuel continued, "And I can't believe Aeric is dead."

Alicia looked down. She didn't know what to say. Samuel attempted to break the silence by changing the subject.

"What have you been doing since I last saw you?"

Alicia extended her hand. "I'm getting married!" She showed him her ring.

"You're what?" Samuel's voice wheezed. "To whom? When?"

"To Philip. We haven't set a date yet." Her joyful countenance turned to confusion. "You seem…surprised?"

"Um, yes. Surprised indeed." Samuel's heart sank. "I didn't even know you were courting."

"Well, only briefly," she said. "It's only been a few weeks." Alicia took a deep breath and smiled brightly. "We are in love. I guess we saw no reason to prolong our courtship."

"When did he ask?" Samuel mustered a half smile.

"First thing this morning."

Samuel turned his gaze from her. "And your father, how does he feel?"

"He's thrilled. You seem…"

"Just surprised. That's all," Samuel said. "It was sudden. And unexpected."

"I should leave you to rest." Alicia stood. "I'm sure you must need it. I can't believe how well you're doing," she spluttered. She always spoke hurriedly when she was uncomfortable. "No one knew how soon you would come out of this. If at all. It's a miracle. I'll go tell your grandfather. He should know that you've awoken."

"That's unnecessary," said a voice at the door. "Samuel, look at you! How wonderful! Praise God Almighty!"

"Good to see you too, Grandfather." Samuel smiled.

Alicia, grateful for the timing of Sir Zachariah's entrance, slipped out of the room without saying goodbye.

The king's men had flown back and forth several times above the ravine and found nothing. They landed at the bottom of a narrow valley where the thick forest crested over them and the gorge snaked sharply. The king hoped this was a safe spot.

The knights and commonlears took the opportunity once again to have their fill of the refreshing water, although they still seemed eager to hunt.

"This doesn't seem right," King Jared whispered to Sir Brendan. "There should be at least one worgraith around here somewhere. The one that killed Aeric—where is it?"

"I wonder if one of the other groups found it yet," Sir Brendan said.

"I don't know." The king let out a quick breath. "Or the worgraiths may have gone into hibernation already. That means we could infiltrate their dens. That might make finishing things a lot easier for us, allowing us to move quickly—and safely."

"I hope you're right," Sir Brendan said. "If that's the case, then we just need to find their lairs."

Downstream, Aiden had bent down on both knees and cupped his hands in the icy water. He sharply drew them back. Aiden looked over at Lucy. She was slurping up the bitingly cold water so fast it was as if she had found an oasis in the desert.

Aiden peered around. The other knights gulped down a few handfuls of water and splashed their faces with it. None of them seemed bothered.

After all, it was just like his training—enduring all weather conditions. Aiden quickly submerged his hands into the piercing cold water. It hurt, but he held his hands there for a moment. He lifted his stinging, shaking hands up to his mouth. His lips curled.

Aiden discovered he was thirstier than he thought, so he swished the water around in his mouth. Shooting pain filled his teeth, but at least the dryness left. He swallowed, and the pain lingered. It was worth it. Aiden drank another scoopful, wiped what felt like ice forming on his face.

Aiden walked over to Lucy and gently placed his hand on her neck as she lapped the frigid water. "What do you suspect, Lucy? We haven't seen one yet. I don't get it. If they travel in packs, where are they? Was there just one lone worgraith?"

Lucy stopped drinking and let out a whine. Then she lifted her head up and gazed at Aiden with a pitiful look.

"You just want to go home, don't you, girl? I don't blame you. I hope they went somewhere far away." But he doubted that very much.

Sir Philip reclined in his father's lounge along with several of his followers, who were finishing off a third bottle of dark, dragon-blood wine. The other two thousand men in Sir Slade's charge were lounging safely elsewhere inside or not far away from Lord Donovan's manor.

"Do you think they're dead yet?" Sir Slade inquired.

"Not all of them," Sir Philip replied. "Not yet."

"How long is this supposed to take?" Sir Slade asked, the alcohol making him bolder than he ought toward Philip. "I don't want the king to get suspicious. It shouldn't appear that we're taking our sweet time searching this tiny part of the glen." He wiped the last of the wine from his mouth onto his forearm.

"Don't worry; there are plenty of worgraiths," the young Sir Philip said. "The king should stumble upon at least one. I just hope Sir Graehme doesn't foul things up," he added spitefully. "He could die, too, though, for all I care."

"You don't trust Sir Graehme?" Sir Jonathan asked.

"He's pathetic. I need someone with commitment, enthusiasm, loyalty to the cause." Philip's speech slurred. He slammed the table with his fist. "I'm hoping this incident with the latest and enhanced breed of worgraiths will force him to live up to the deal. If he doesn't…"

Sir Philip looked around the table. His eyes narrowed. It seemed as if someone else was looking through those eyes. Someone unrecognizable. Someone more evil than anyone they had seen before. It was as if he were possessed. "He'll die a ghastly death like the rest of them." Philip took the last swig of wine.

"But you're right, Slade." He wiped his mouth on his glove. "We must leave soon. It must not appear we have been lazy. We must be shocked and horrified at what we will discover." He looked around the table again, seeming to return to himself. "But we must do so at the right time. We must arrive after it is too late to save them."

"And how will we know that we, too, won't be fodder for the worgraiths?" Sir Slade asked with a hint of doubt in his voice.

"I have a guaranteed protection," Sir Philip replied as he stared maliciously at Slade. "Remember," a low voice slithered from Philip's lips, "I have The Power Within."

"Alright men, gather around," Sir Brendan bellowed as he walked through the biting, shallow waters of Spring Creek. "The king has some important information. Leave your commonlears where they are. Come along, gather 'round."

The gentle rhythm of the quietly bubbling creek had calmed Lucy enough that she lay rather peacefully. Aiden, leaning his back against her, finished an apple, threw its core to the side, and languidly stood to meet his father.

"Gentlemen," the king said as the knights assembled, "let me say that as your ruler, I am honored by the bravery, courage, discipline, and respect you have displayed on this task. I think it is safe to assume that we have all expected to have encountered fierce battle with at least one worgraith by now. And I suspect that all of you are wondering why, just as I am, that we have not." The men didn't seem to respond with any particular expression. "It is my belief, as it is Sir Brendan's and a few others whom I've just talked with, that the worgraiths may have already gone into hibernation."

A few men nodded in agreement.

"Usually, this species doesn't hibernate until after the first snowfall. But, as we expect the snow to fall any day, perhaps they have already found and settled in their lairs. If so, then this will make our task easier, and we will then be able to go home relatively unscathed." The king looked around. He saw no change in the men's mood—no fear, no disappointment, no excitement. "Although we have the daunting task of searching for their dens, we can kill while they lie dormant. This opportunity, I believe, is a gift from God, Who is acting mercifully on our behalf."

Now the men gave a silent, unified smile and nod.

"We will just simply have to search as many caves as possible. This area is notorious for its caves—large, winding caves, many not fully explored."

King Jared thought for a moment. Only several of the men standing before him had experience exploring these caves. "We'll start with the cave behind Upper Falls. Since it's the largest cave, we can easily assume it is now a worgraith's lair."

A knight asked, "Your majesty, what about Sir Graehme's and Sir Slade's troops?"

"We must send an envoy. Aiden will search for Sir Slade's men; I will tell Sir Graehme. I am assigning Sir Brendan to your charge until I return. We begin immediately. Good luck, and God be with us all."

A sudden roar surged among the mighty men as they raised their fists in the air and bellowed—ready to fight, and ready to win.

Six

"I don't remember pulling myself up onto shore," Samuel said, "or certainly anything that happened after that. All I remember is I was slipping. I couldn't hang on…That's it." Samuel stared into space. "That's all I remember."

His eyes widened in panic.

"Savannah…what happened to Savannah? Is she alright?"

Zachariah's countenance, already pale and grave from listening to his grandson's story, withered even more. The overflowing joy he had felt when he first entered the room and laid eyes on his grandson had slipped away as he listened to the horrors his only remaining family member had endured. *I knew a time would come when my beloved grandson would have to face these kinds of things. But it has all come too fast* he thought. "No, Samuel. She died—at the hands of the beast."

Samuel's eyes filled with tears as he tried to not weep. But his emotions got the best of him.

It was time.

Sir Philip gathered his men, thankful no one had gotten into some kind of drunken brawl or ruined any of his father's furnishings and headed them out to find the whereabouts of the king's men.

By this time, dark clouds had overtaken the morning sky. A brisk wind with a spittle of rain seeped into their bones. But it was a mere inconvenience. Philip nearly licked his lips in anticipation of seeing the corpses of the king and prince—that is, if the worgraiths had not consumed them yet.

"There, what's that?" Slade asked, pointing to what appeared to be a shadowy commonlear and knight quietly breaking through the mist and drizzle up ahead.

Philip took out a telescope he'd stolen from his father's house.

"It looks like the king's son," Philip said, his face drawn. He paused. *This wasn't right,* he thought. *What is he doing alone and why is he approaching this way? Maybe he's the lone survivor of an attack.* Philip's heart stirred. Something convinced him that although Aiden was alive, everything would proceed as planned. Just give it time. The Power is at work.

"Slade, keep to the plan," Philip commanded.

It didn't take long before Philip and his group met up with Aiden. "I take it you must not have found any, either. Your men seem unscathed," Aiden said.

"That's right," Sir Slade said. "We searched Lord Donovan's glen thoroughly. There were no worgraiths there, thankfully. What about the men in your group?"

"We have not seen any, either. My father has gone to find Sir Graehme's group. Hopefully, they're fine, too. Father decided we should hunt down the worgraiths in their lairs. They've probably started hibernating."

Sir Slade glanced over at Sir Philip, who slowly and discreetly nodded.

"Good plan," Sir Slade said. "That's fine."

"Good. Come on; I'll show you where we're to meet."

Aiden bore his heels into Lucy's side, snapped her reins, and led Sir Slade's group to the protected portion of the gorge he had just left.

The rain came down in heavy sheets that would have stung if it weren't for the armor. Though the rain was cold, Philip was hot with anger.

It couldn't be my fault; I did everything perfectly, he thought. *Was there a problem with these worgraiths? Did they not breed properly?*

"Master," Philip whispered, "what went wrong?"

A deep, dark swirl flowed through his heart. He heard his master's voice whisper back, "A minor setback. It was nothing. Just proceed."

Samuel's physician, Sir James, confirmed what Zachariah, Alicia, and Samuel already knew. Samuel was doing unusually well, considering the circumstances. But because of the tender aches he felt all over, Sir James still advised bed rest until at least morning.

"You'll be sore for a while," the doctor said. "You'll walk with a limp, probably, for the next day or two. But otherwise, you're in miraculously fine condition for someone who fell into a pool of jagged rocks."

"Praise God," Zachariah said. His spirit lifted once again.

"Are you hungry?" the doctor asked. He peered out the window, measuring the time of day against the sun, which was hard to see considering the rainy, overcast sky.

"Not really," Samuel held his stomach.

"Maybe in a little while." The doctor turned back to Samuel and wrote something down in a small book. "I don't know what the cooks have planned, but it smells wonderful, like some sort of hearty soup with fresh bread."

"Oh, well…maybe I could have a little," Samuel said.

"Considering it's nearly midday, it should be ready any time." Sir James walked to the door. "I'll have them send it up as soon as it's prepared. I'll be back to see you before nightfall. Please, there are nurses available at your call. Don't hesitate to ring that bell if you need something."

Samuel glanced over to where the head physician was pointing. On a table next to his bed was a small bell. "Hmph." Samuel gave the bell a subtle ring. "I never noticed that was there."

"Well, now you have. Don't hesitate to use it. Good day."

"Good day," Samuel and Zachariah replied in unison.

Within moments, Samuel rang the bell loud and clear. Zachariah cocked his head and gave his grandson a puzzled look.

"I need to use the lavatory," he said. "Badly."

"Oh," Zachariah said, tilting his head back with a smirk. "You know, there are a lot of pretty nurses here. I'm sure that will at least be somewhat comforting while you stay."

"Let's hope so," Samuel said.

The sound of scuffing shoes echoed in the hallway. The steps stopped just inside Samuel's door. A woman wearing a long, white gown entered the room. She was unpleasantly plump and had wrinkles on her forehead and around her dark, saggy, bloodshot eyes. Her wide nose was warty, her teeth were askew, and she bore a few moles. Her somewhat-managed brown hair stuck out around her head.

"Yes?" she grumbled.

"Um, can you help me up, please?"

She let out a moan and rolled her eyes.

Samuel looked over at his grandfather. They both tried hard to stifle a laugh, but it was no use. Samuel hurt as he chuckled, but it was worth it. It felt good to laugh a little. The nurse seemed not to notice it was about her.

Through the haze of rain, King Jared saw the shadows of half of the men assigned to Sir Graehme approaching in the distance. The king halted Enoch in midair and waited for the group to come to him. Observing them through his telescope, the king could see many injured men, their garments and heavy armor bloodied and damaged, matching the wounds on their commonlears.

He noticed that all seemed solemn and grim, hunched on their commonlears, exhausted, hopeless—an all too familiar sign of retreat.

King Jared noticed Sir Graehme mildly perk when he saw his king waiting before him. He straightened his slumping posture, as did many others who took notice of their king.

The king set his shoulders back and lifted his chin. King Jared took a deep breath and puffed out his chest. With effort, he mustered a slight grin. His eyes emitted a signal of pride and satisfaction in his men's gallantry.

"Halt!" Sir Graehme commanded. He was the first to bend forward to a bow, and his men followed suit.

After their bow, the men postured like the soldiers their king had seen before they left for this grim battle. The rain suddenly fell hard.

"We have lost many men, your majesty," Sir Graehme shouted. The rain clanked on their armor. "As you can see. It was from one worgraith."

"One?" the king asked, his mouth agape and eyes suddenly wide. "How can this be?"

Sir Graehme answered, "This breed—it's like no other. Not like the ones we've fought before, Your Majesty. These worgraiths can cast fire from their mouths."

King Jared's eyes grew large. Then, with a scowl, he leaned his head toward Sir Graehme. "Fire-breathing dragons?"

"That's right, your majesty."

Dear God, help us. Why had Aiden not said anything about that?

"The battle was short," Sir Graehme continued. "We would have tried to find you sooner, but we waited until the beast had left the scene so that it was safe for our return. It took a while for it to leave, considering we had blinded it." A smile stretched across his face. "We then finished attending to the wounded. Many men and commonlears died after the battle, your majesty—from their wounds. We took it upon ourselves to bury them where they lay"

"Come," the king said. "Let me take you to a safe place. There, I will tell you the next step to our plan. Your men have fought honorably. I am proud of you, each and every one. You will all receive a special commendation when we return home."

About the time Aiden and Philip's crew got back to the meeting place, the stinging rain had subsided into a cold mist. A dark cloud kept a shadow over the land. Aiden sat on a rock at the water's edge, throwing stones into the creek; he could sense two men walking toward him. It was Philip and Slade.

"We want to talk with you," Slade said.

"What about?" Aiden responded sharply.

"The plan—" Slade replied, "What is it?"

Aiden's tension eased, seeing that they meant no harm. "Father reassigned his men to search the cave at Upper Falls under Sir Brendan's leadership until he returns from gathering Sir Graehme's forces." Aiden skipped a stone across the creek. It clapped against the stony gorge wall on the other side. "We think the worgraiths may have gone into hibernation. I don't know what he wants to do with your group, exactly. He didn't say." Aiden skipped another stone across the creek.

"So, if we find these things hibernating, we just go in, slice them up, and that's that? No problem?" Philip said.

"That's the plan," Aiden replied. He so desperately wanted to get away from these two.

"An interesting idea," Philip said. "But do you know for sure if they're hibernating?"

"No, but I guess we'll find out," Aiden said.

"I guess we will," Philip said slowly and softly as his eyes bore deep into Aiden. A crooked smirk crossed his face.

Aiden noticed Philip's strange tone. A voice shouted, "The king is coming!" Aiden rose. The sun broke through the clouds behind King Jared and Sir Graehme's men, enveloping them in a misty beam of light.

Aiden put one hand to his brow to shield the sunlight from his eyes. *What happened?* he asked, noticing the bloodied and ragged men.

"Looks like they've seen battle," Sir Slade said with a hint of glee. "Come on, let's find out what happened." Slade and Philip ran to Sir Graehme's crew, shoving aside others who were also hurrying to greet the battle-worn men.

Aiden tossed the rest of his pebbles aside and shook his head in disgust. By the time he had walked over, the drizzle had fully stopped. A brisk wind gently swept the canyon. Aiden shivered. How he wished he could warm himself by the fire, have some hot soup and change into dry clothes.

King Jared dismounted Enoch and barely waited for all of his men to gather before he spoke. "Men, we are at war with something much greater than what we had expected. It seems some other, more dangerous breed of worgraith has made its way to Whiterock. These beasts can cast fire from their mouths."

Aiden instantly heard a few quiet gasps and sighs around him. Sir Slade and Sir Philip caught his attention. They looked at each other and seemed to stifle an excitement.

The sun peeked evermore through the clouds, bringing much-needed warmth with it. The king continued, "We have to be very careful, very perceptive when we search. I hope to God that these things truly are hibernating."

Sir Philip asked, "My King, what if they are not hibernating? Is there a backup plan?"

"Fight," King Jared said. "Fight with all your might." The king peered around. "Men, are we ready?"

"Yes, sir!" they answered.

"Then let us find them, by the power of God Almighty! And slaughter the wretched beasts into extinction once and for all!"

A mild cheer erupted from the members of Sir Slade's group as an angry shout of revenge broke out from Sir Graehme's lot.

"I want Sir Slade's army to split into two squadrons—the first squad to be two-thirds of your men, and the second squad to be one third. Since Sir Graehme's forces are heavily diminished, they could use two-thirds of your men. Divide them as you wish, Sir Slade, but I want Philip in the second squad, and that squad will come with me."

Aiden's heart sank. But of course, his father would have to choose Philip.

"It will be my privilege, Your Majesty." Philip bowed before the king, his eyes catching Aiden's. "I will certainly do what is necessary to make sure nothing prevents me from being successful to my call."

As Philip approached Sir Graehme, anger welled all the more with each step. Trying to keep his voice low, Sir Phillip said, "Have you forgotten you've sworn allegiance to The Power Within? You were not to harm any worgraiths. You were to avoid going into the glen altogether and come back with your men unharmed, telling the king that the worgraiths are nowhere to be found."

Graehme's voice shook. "Sorry sir, but not everyone on my squad is a member of The Power Within. They would have asked questions, incriminated us, and then exposed the plan. I thought it best to obey the king—"

"*I* am your king!" Philip whispered loudly.

"But King Jared and Prince Aiden are not dead yet," Graehme said. "Until the worgraiths have killed them and you are on the throne, I cannot take the chance of—"

"Any informants against you would have had to answer to me! I would have pardoned any punishment Jared would have laid against you once I took his throne in just a few fleeting days!" Philip clenched his teeth. The flames of Hell pierced through his eyes and bore into Graehme. "Mark my words: the king and his son will not return from this mission alive."

Sir Graehme's voice shook even more. "Until I can confirm with absolute certainty that my king and my prince are dead, I will obey their orders…"

Philip smacked Graehme across the face with his gloves. "You have your orders from *me!*" He stared at Graehme, incensed. Then, with a few deep breaths, Philip changed his demeanor. "Perhaps you are right," he said cooly. "Maybe it would be best if you obeyed *your* king."

Philip turned and walked towards his squadron, ready for flight. He mumbled some sort of foreign, almost ancient language that came to him during moments when he would incant blessings of protection on the Power's followers and curses on their enemies. Turning to look at Graehme once he finished his spell, Philip's sinister smile and forceful glare told Graehme that something was about to happen—to him.

"Surely I've not just made myself an enemy of The Power Within," Sir Graehme whispered aloud. "After all, I'm riding alongside Sir Slade. What could possibly go wrong?"

"Have you spotted anything unusual?" King Jared asked as soon as he and Aiden, along with Philip and his crew, landed in the wooded overhang across from Upper Falls.

"No," Sir Brendan replied. "We've waited here observing, just as you had commanded. The falls are as they have always been— quiet and peaceful."

"Then let's go. There is no time to waste."

"Yes, Your Majesty," Sir Brendan said.

King Jared had ordered half of his squadron to hover on their commonlears in a semi-circular formation outside the cave halfway between the falls and the gorge wall, bows in hand.

In the event a worgraith escaped the blockade, the other half of the king's men formed additional barriers further along the gorge in either direction. Sir Philip's men waited in a standby position in a wooded outlook on the top of a cliff across from the falls. Though fallen leaves had prevented them from being well-concealed, the king hoped they were still masked well enough.

King Jared led a small group of men, which included Aiden, Sir Brendan, Sir Jonathan, Sir Philip, and a dozen others, to a natural walkway that led to the cave.

Taking the rear of the line, Sir Jonathan whispered to Sir Philip, "What is your plan, Your Majesty?"

"Cousin, my plan is simply to watch them die. Be thankful that you are privileged enough to be by my side to see this happen."

"Forgive me, My Lord, but are you sure the plan will work this time?" Sir Jonathan winced. "What if the worgraith really is hibernating? What if it doesn't attack? After all, the king and his son should have already been dead by now."

With a mix of agitation and a hint of delight, Philip replied, "Perhaps the Great Power willed for us to see our adversary die right before our eyes. The Great Power is gracious to his people. His ways are always perfect. Have faith, my friend."

As if reciting scripture, Sir Jonathan, with a sinister glee in his voice, said, "Oh what grace our god endows."

The men lifted their shields above their heads and made their way through the freezing cold waterfall into the cool cave behind. The men felt as if they had been showered with tiny ice pellets.

None of this seemed to bother the commonlears, however.

King Jared removed his torch from a pouch attached to Enoch's saddle, hoping that the waterfall hadn't ruined it. The other men followed suit. It wasn't long before the king successfully lit his torch with the use of some flint, and each of the soldiers lit theirs with the passing of King Jared's flame.

The ground was wet and slick, and within a matter of just a few steps, it also became dangerously steep. Aiden's torch flickered in a brief cool wind that whisked through the cavern. He shivered slightly.

"Watch out; this seems to only be getting steeper," the king said, trying to keep his voice low. He stopped his men then stepped a few paces away. The light from his torch magnifying the quivering of the king's hand revealed a sharp cliff that delved into an abyss. The king trembled more as he took hold of Enoch's reins for support and leaned over just a little more.

"How deep is it?" Aiden asked.

"I'm…not sure. I cannot see the bottom."

Peering westward down the canyon, Sir Graehme checked to see what they were up against. "There's two of them. It looks like one is a brown-blonde and the other is the black one we blinded," Sir Graehme said. "Both worgraiths are sitting on the bottom of the ravine. The blind dragon slumps, as if it's given up all hope of living. The other is looking over him caringly, as if it's his mate."

With a face like stone, Sir Slade asked, "Are your men ready?"

"Absolutely." Sir Graehme said.

"Then let's divide and conquer. I'll give your men the privilege of first strike—for retribution's sake."

Sir Graehme nodded, put on his helmet, and raised his sword in the air. "For Whiterock!"

"For Whiterock!" Sir Graehme's men roared, lifting their swords high in the air.

Sir Graehme then pointed his sword at the two worgraiths. "Onward! Attack!" Graehme's troops surged with a great bellow, their dragons moving with vast speed and force.

As the sound of the soldier's fury reached the beasts, the blinded worgraith perked up while the other rose with vengeance in its stare. It drew back its shoulders and planted its feet.

"Stop. Do you hear something?" King Jared whispered to Aiden.

As the king and his son brought the line to a halt, Aiden listened intently, waiting. "No," he whispered.

"I hear movement, like a battle going on, not far away," said the king. "But it doesn't sound like a worgraith. It sounds more human, but it's hard to tell."

He looked toward the sound and unsheathed his sword. The high-pitched sound of scraping metal on metal and inarticulate guttural yells reverberated through the cave. "There, do you hear it now?"

"I do!" Aiden said.

Splash! Another soldier had fallen, the canyon littered with blood-soaked, lifeless men and slaughtered commonlears. Fire erupted everywhere, it seemed, as men fought to stay out of the blaze that poured from the two worgraiths' mouths.

Sir Graehme once again felt the urge to order a retreat as he witnessed the number of his men diminish before his eyes. He looked everywhere for Sir Slade's men; they were nowhere to be found. His men alone raged against two beasts. He was trapped. He knew he would not come out of this alive.

"Order us in!" Sir Slade heard one of his men. "What's going on? Why are we not fighting?"

"We have our orders from our lord," Sir Slade said. "Graehme still shows loyalty to King Jared. He must be dealt with—he and his entire army. We'll let the worgraiths do their job. We only need to make sure he and his men don't leave here alive."

"I can't watch men of The Order die!" the soldier said. "Our bond is sacred; we're sworn to protect each other to the death. Are you out of your mind?"

Sir Slade glared at his insolent soldier and recited a foreign incantation. Then he said, "If any of you are brave enough to tackle the furious monsters, do so at your own risk."

After a brief pause, the audacious knight charged ahead. Several other knights followed. Sir Slade and the rest of his men watched as the subordinates chose death instead of life. One by one, a few more flew out from Sir Slade's regiment, choosing to fight alongside Sir Graehme.

Slade turned to face his men. "Gentlemen, whom do you serve, The Power or the grave?" Sir Slade turned back around to watch his enemies' destruction.

Zigzagging his commonlear to avoid being caught and torn into shreds, Sir Graehme's arrows added to the many of those sunken deep into the monster. It did not shriek, but the more pain it received, the more it grit its teeth and snarled.

The flapping of wings and battle cries drew Sir Graehme's attention as a contingent of Slade's men joined the fight alongside their brethren. With a renewed vigor, Graehme charged the great beast head on. He swerved his commonlear to avoid a blaze coming toward him. He slipped off the saddle but kept a tight grip on the reins. It jerked Graehme's commonlear's head and neck. The commonlear spun. Graehme slipped and plunged to his death.

Both worgraiths stood back-to-back, successfully warding off their enemies with their dreadful flames.

Several of Sir Slade's men zoomed between the two monsters' heads. With swords held out, they scraped and tore into the necks of the worgraiths, despite their orders not to harm the creatures. The worgraiths spun, attempting to dislodge their attackers, and along with many of Sir Graehme's men, the two monsters inadvertently set each other on fire. The worgraiths writhed in pain. They both reached for each other as if to beg forgiveness for their horrendous mistake. Their arms locked in a moment of anguished embrace. Then they fell lifeless into Spring Creek, which doused their charred remains.

Graehme's soldiers cheered as Slade's eyes burned with demonic rage. He bared his teeth like a mad dog. There was only one thing left to do now.

— ⚔ —

Light rebounded off the wet walls of the deep and treacherous cavern, shimmering as if made of glass. King Jared advanced his men further into the wide underground. But they had not gotten far before the sound of footprints scuffing against rock and dirt, thuds against the ground, blades clashing, and eerie voices in the utter darkness had caused them to press forward with extreme caution.

The trail narrowed, which meant the deep overhang to their side was ever closer, and it still seemed bottomless. King Jared slipped and fell hard.

"Father, are you alright?"

"Yes, I'm fine," the king groaned.

Aiden helped him up. "Do you want to rest?"

"No, no," King Jared said, arching his back, "we must press on."

Sir Brendan said, "Your majesty, another passage. There to the right. Should we take it?"

"Perhaps we should split up," a voice from the back piped.

"Philip?" the king asked as he moved his torch toward the voice. "Was that you?"

"Yes, Your Majesty."

The king's eyes lit up. "You think we should split up?"

"Yes, Sire. We don't know which tunnel the worgraith's lair might be in."

"But there's strength in numbers. I'd hate…" The king paused and lowered his head for a moment. "Yes, I think you might be right. After all, we're here to scout. We'll send for the others once we find the dragon's lair."

"I'll take half through this tunnel to the right," Sir Brendan volunteered. "Your majesty, would you like to come with me? It looks as if the footing is…"

"No, no. I think it's time we take flight. After all, that's why our commonlears are here."

"As you wish, your majesty," Sir Brendan replied. He turned, lifted his torch in the air, and pointed. "You, six. Follow me."

Sir Philip lifted his torch. "The rest of us would be proud to accompany our king," he said.

King Jared warmly smiled. "Thank you, Sir Philip. Your loyalty is greatly appreciated."

Aiden clenched his jaw and tightened his fist.

Turning to Sir Brendan, King Jared said, "Good luck and Godspeed."

"The Almighty will be with us," Sir Brendan added.

"I believe so," the king replied.

With renewed vigor, the king and his knights mounted their steeds. Their faithful dragons cautiously but swiftly flew their masters through the deep, dark tunnels. The cold, damp cave and rush of wind only exacerbated Aiden's sour mood. Even with a torch by his side, he had not fully warmed from the icy waterfall. Now, with Sir Brendan and his men separated, he had to contend with Philip and endure his father's sickening admiration for him.

Sir Slade's army hovered in midair, their dragons' wings beating with a heavy rhythm that matched the rage that flowed like molten lava through Slade's blood. Sir Graehme's troops had prematurely celebrated their victory as they passed each other in a triumphant circle that reminded Sir Slade of flies in a pasture. These pesky knights would soon meet their intended doom. Just not as Slade's master had originally planned. The remnant of Sir Slade's soldiers drastically outnumbered the dissenting knights who fought by Sir Graehme's side.

Sir Matthew, who had assumed command after Sir Graehme died, flew to Sir Slade. "I demand to know why you did not fight! Who are you to disobey the order of our king? Only a traitor or a coward would defy King Jared!"

"Strong words, commander." Sir Slade said. "Do you think your small band of faithful knights can compare to the supremacy of The Power Within?"

"The only power I know is that of our God and king!"

"Then prepare to meet them." Sir Slade lifted his sword and shouted a strange war cry as he cracked the reins of his commonlear, kicked his boots into its side, and charged forward to duel Sir Matthew.

With a rousing shout, angry soldiers soon followed as Sir Slade's army descended upon Sir Matthew's tiny group of men. The two armies clashed into each other with bitter force. Sir Slade's blade clashed against Sir Matthew's, and the two fought as their fierce commonlears bit at each other's necks, ripping flesh and armor, spinning in the air, and tumbling to the floor below.

Sir Matthew's men fought bravely, but their diminished numbers could not stand against the swarm of soldiers fighting like killer bees angrily guarding their hive.

The indiscernible noises King Jared heard moments ago echoed louder. He halted Enoch and his line of men. A loud roar reverberated from not far ahead. "Those screams are from commonlears—and men!" King Jared said. "We have no time to send for reinforcements. We must forge ahead!"

Philip's evil smile sickened Aiden.

"Remember the vital importance of this mission," King Jared said. "For our homes and our people, for Whiterock and our children's children!" The king unsheathed his sword. His men did the same.

Aiden petted Lucy on the side and stroked her neck. Her muscles were tight, and her breathing was quick. Aiden leaned in. "It's alright," he whispered. "We did this once before. We can do it again—especially with more by our side." Lucy's breathing calmed, but she was still tense.

The commonlears flew into the darkness with a swift hush. Up ahead, the cavern lit with a fiery red glow. The men heard another roar, but despite the glow, no one could see a worgraith. Commonlears weaved around the stalactites and stalagmites as screams echoed through the cavern. The crimson glow and the shadows it produced moved and swayed.

Off to the right, as the cavern walls turned to expose the unseen, the warriors finally saw a mighty beast and Sir Brendan's men caught in a fight.

Riding their commonlears around the great creature, Sir Brendan's men held onto their torches with one hand while swinging their swords with the other. Those who used arrows had tossed their torches to the ground.

"Men! *Charge!*" The king yelled. Faster they flew. The monster hurled commonlears left and right. Arrows dotted the monster, yet the great beast fought as though the stinging arrows did not exist. Commonlears swerved to avoid capture.

Aiden recognized this worgraith as the one that killed Aeric. Revenge settled in his heart. Nothing was going to stop him now. He had battled this thing once before and survived. Now, he would not let *it* survive. It stood with knees and arms bent, feet firmly in place. Its shoulders were back, and its wings spread out. It spewed flames all around, the heat nearly unbearable.

Aiden noticed that the torches scurrying around the worgraith presented an easy target, which gave him an idea. Perhaps there was a way to obtain reinforcements.

EIGHT

Though it hadn't been long, Alicia found herself drawn to visit Samuel again. As she walked through the corridors of the recovery center, her mind stirred over his reaction to her recent engagement. It wasn't what she expected. Sure, she had Aiden to contend with, but he'd get over it in time. Samuel, on the other hand—if Samuel didn't get over his seeming dislike for Philip, she might never see him again. She wouldn't want that to happen. Alicia knocked on Samuel's door.

"Oh, good. I think I have my appetite back." Samuel said.

Barely able to hold back her laughter, she replied, "Goat's bladder soup. Your favorite, I'm told."

"Awwhgh! Who in the world told you…"

She peeked her head through the door and smiled warmly. Her heart lifted as it always had when she joked around with him.

"It's you!" he said with a smile.

Alicia giggled as she walked in.

"Sir, I thought we weren't supposed to go up against these things," one of Philip's men complained. "I thought you said…"

"I never promised that you wouldn't have to face one; I simply promised protection. Don't worry; you have a covering from The Power. Now go do as your commander tells you!"

Sir Philip and Sir Jonathan joined the fight, and as The Power had promised them, the mighty worgraith did not lay its hands on them.

"Father," Aiden pleaded. "I know it will work. We have to try."

"I think it's a worthy idea," Sir Brendan said.

"Alright," the king said. "The both of you, help me call the men." The king gave a deep breath as his eyes regained their spark. "I hope this works." He whipped Enoch's reins.

The three sped off on their commonlears and waved their torches back and forth. "Fall back! Fall back!" they shouted. "Gather near the king!"

Sir Philip and Sir Jonathan looked at each other, dumbfounded by this command to retreat. Without a word, they joined the rest of the troops. Sir Brendan and Aiden fought with all of their might to keep the beast distracted while the king gave the knights a quick command. In a moment's time, they had flown back to the beast and engaged in combat. Sir Philip's men buzzed around the worgraith but avoided actually harming his precious creation.

Brendan and Aiden had flown their commonlears directly into the beast's face. They clawed and gnawed on its flesh as Aiden and Brendan jabbed it with their torches. The worgraith grabbed Brendan and his commonlear and threw them. Brendan held on and regained flight. Aiden sensed he was next. "Lucy, go! Quick! Move!"

The beast caught Lucy and Aiden in its hand and ripped them off of its face. It roared in pain as Lucy held on with all her might, gashing the mighty giant's skin open with her talons. In one swift move, it quickly caught the king with its other hand.

Philip smiled.

Sir Brendan gave a hearty battle cry once more and waved his torch furiously to catch the evil beast's attention. "Over here, you monster! Over here!

As the creature turned around, Sir Brendan took in the lifeless forms of his king, his prince, and their commonlears, clutched in the monster's hands. Sir Brendan's jaw dropped. His heart stopped. His head spun. He had to shake his mind from the awful tragedy. Sir Brendan turned sharply and led the troops as fast as he could away from the beast.

The worgraith laid his catch down, limp as rag dolls, on the floor of his lair and chased after the others, not wanting the rest of his food to escape. The worgraith screamed furiously as it ran toward them.

"Dear God, don't let them die in vain," Sir Brendan said. "Lord, please be with us! Let this plan work! If I must die, too, so be it, but see this plan through to completion!" The commonlears zoomed their masters through the dark and treacherous tunnel.

The soldiers guarding the entrance to Upper Falls had succumbed to boredom. They had sat there staring at a waterfall in silence for much too long. The men had stretched their legs and backs as best as they could while still sitting on their commonlears, but still everything below their waists had numbed, and their backs ached. They cracked their necks and had tried not to draw too much attention to themselves as they yawned. The men had to force themselves not to hunch in their saddles, achingly trying to sit upright while bearing the weight of their armor. The commonlears, too, seemed to sway up and down a bit more; their wings needed rest.

SPLA-WHOOSH!

A sudden burst of colors splashed out from behind the waterfall. The watchmen and their dragons jumped. The men quickly tried to regain hold of their commonlears with all their might as their steeds panicked. But it was useless. Though the knights flew swiftly past them, the worgraith's mighty momentum caused it to fly into the sentry, knocking many others aside and into the canyon wall. As if it didn't care or notice a host of new prey, the worgraith continued to follow its attackers down the canyon, where a second set of guards waited.

As the knights regained control of their commonlears, they pursued the savage beast from behind as the knights further down the ravine attacked head on.

The onslaught of men and beasts was relentless, and nothing stood in the way of the furious attack on this monster.

It landed, took a firm stance, and spread its wings. The worgraith furrowed its brows and bared its teeth. It roared, swatted its arms, swung its mighty tail, and cast fire from its mouth, but this did not hamper the king's mighty men. They attacked the monster from head to toe. The worgraith lifted off the ground and spun around in every direction, shooting flames that dropped men into the bottom of the gorge like sparks from forging metal.

Sir Brendan gnashed his teeth, his eyes full of tears, his voice full of rage, his mind in shock over the creature's quick and easy murder of his beloved king and prince. Sir Brendan resolved himself to be the knight that slays this dragon. Indeed, no one fought the beast more bravely or harder than he. Using the same tactic that he and Aiden used in the cave, Sir Brendan's commonlear flew straight for its face, gashing it into shreds. Sir Brendan still had his torch. Although the waterfall had doused its flame, he sunk it into the creature's face.

The next thing Sir Brendan knew, the worgraith had caught him tightly within its grasp. "Aarrgh! Someone…loosen its grip!" He saw members of Lord Donovan's garrison around him. "Sir Philip! Jonathan! Slade! Someone!"

With a nod, Sir Philip flew around to the worgraith's hands, but signaled to Jonathan and Slade not to do anything.

The worgraith snapped out its arm. It clutched Sir Slade and his commonlear. "No!" Sir Jonathan screamed.

"Get it…get it, Jonathan…get it to open its fist!" Sir Slade called, gasping for air. Jonathan's commonlear clutched the worgraith's wrist and dug into its veins. Jonathan jabbed his sword into its wrist, piercing an artery. The sting caused the creature to open its hand, but the beast swung its arm sharply, throwing Sir Slade and his commonlear into the canyon wall. Stunned, Sir Jonathan and his commonlear fell downward and splashed into a deep pocket in the creek.

"No!" Sir Philip yelled, angry at his creation's failure. "No! I commanded a covering! You were not to harm *any* of *my* people! You will pay for your carelessness! I made you; I will destroy you!" Philip clenched his jaws and drew his arm back for a menacing blow. He sliced the animal's other wrist with ease, freeing Sir Brendan.

The animal went down on its knees with commonlears still buzzing around it. The worgraith slumped over, face first. Its blood poured into Spring Creek.

"What happened, My Lord? What happened?" Philip beseeched the Power.

On a shaded cliff just above the battle site, Sir Brendan had landed his commonlear and gazed over the ravine. Every bit of energy and hope drained from his mind. He dismounted his dragon, walked a few paces toward the edge in silence, and turned his head away from the horrific sight. The tightening in his heart unraveled after a few deep breaths.

Sir Brendan went back to his commonlear, saddled, and flew to a gathering of men near the worgraith below. He landed behind Sir Philip, who was standing in a pool of water and blood. Though he could not see Sir Philip's expression, Philip seemed fixated on the massive worgraith. Just within arm's reach of the mighty beast, Sir Philip had one hand on his commonlear's reins, the other hand fisted hard against his mouth. Sir Brendan didn't bother to dismount.

With as much strength in his voice as he could muster, he said, "Men, attend to the wounded. We are going back to the castle. Do not delay. We must take the injured to the recovery center immediately, and we must tell everyone that the king and his son are dead. We must prepare for their remains to be appropriately transported back to the castle."

Sir Brendan lowered his voice. "Thank you, Philip. You saved my life. You've saved all of us."

Another wicked smile played across Sir Philip's face. "I...I could not save the king or his son."

Sir Brendan didn't answer, pausing before he spoke again. "Alicia is not of age yet to take over the kingdom," he said, withholding his emotions. "Stewarding the kingdom until she is of age is Zachariah's responsibility, not your father's."

"Understood, Sire. But did you know Alicia and I are betrothed?" Sir Philip turned to face Sir Brendan.

"What?" Sir Brendan replied, "Well, I suppose—after your marriage, then—you'll be our new king."

NINE

Aiden woke, his eyes still closed. There was no sound. The ground was cold, hard, and wet. His eyes shot open.

Darkness.

A deep, massless void spread out like eternity on all sides. Panic gripped his heart. His mind spun. *Am I dead? Is this what it's like to be dead?*

A soft fiery light flickered warmly beyond an opening not far from him. Aiden didn't move a muscle, his ears listening for the slightest noise from the lighted passageway. He heard nothing. Calmness settled over him. *If I'm dead, then this is much better than what I thought hell would be like. No fiery pit, no demons.*

Aiden slowly sat up, dizzy, head pounding. *Ugh—your head must have to adjust to waking up dead,* he thought. *That's odd, but I suppose—it's plausible. After all, I've never known anyone who died and lived to tell about it.*

He eased himself to a stand and took a few unsteady steps, a little nauseous. He walked to the opening in the wall. Something moved. He stopped quickly and slowly peered through the gap.

Wait a minute…my sword. Yes, Aiden still had his sheath wrapped around him. His hands reached for the hilt—not there. *Just like God's sick sense of humor. Send me to Hell with a sheath but no sword. That is, if I'm really dead.*

He looked to his left. An ascending stone ramp led to another open doorway. Past the door, a hallway apparently led off to the right.

Aiden stood there silently, waiting, listening, deciding what to do next. *What was that noise? Was there someone just around that corner? Someone friendly?* Aiden's fear intensified at the horrendous reality that he might *really* be dead and that maybe this dark, lonely, dreaded place was *actually* his inescapable eternity.

Aiden crept up the ramp.

"So, you've awoken."

Aiden jumped. A gigantic man twice his height had suddenly appeared. "I've been waiting for you."

Aiden involuntarily held his breath. He had to will himself to breathe again. If only he had his sword.

The giant creature smiled, gesturing his hand outward, and said, "Come."

Aiden assessed this thing. This enormous individual had an unusual sort of skin and bone texture that Aiden had never seen or heard of before. It was as if this creature were a living bronze statue. But his voice had a wonderful tone—clear and beautiful, as if a trumpet could speak.

His eyes were blue, lit from within, almost as if by fire. And he had long, flowing blond hair. He wore garments that were pure white and shined brightly, the way the sun reflected off freshly fallen snow.

It doesn't seem demonic; it's too angelic. But wait, didn't someone once say that demons were once angels that had rebelled? That Satan masquerades as an Angel of Light? Then certainly this could be a demon.

"Come, Aiden. I need to take you somewhere," the giant said, grinning slowly. "Your destiny awaits."

Take me somewhere—where? And he knows my name!

The massive humanoid extended his hand further to Aiden as he pointed his other huge hand down the narrow corridor, which bent to the left, concealing the mystery of what lay ahead. "I have my orders," he said. "I am your escort."

Escort? Escort into the pit?

The giant stared at him. After a moment, he spoke again. "You must come with me," he said. "You need not fear."

Aiden stepped back. *Not fear? Surely, he must be lying.*

Aiden and the giant remained silent for a moment, looking at each other, waiting for the other's next move. Aiden felt as if he were living in a nightmare. His entire internal being twisted as this thing looked at him. His heart had never pounded like this before. Aiden grabbed a torch and ran back down the ramp into the dark tomb in which he had awoken.

"Aiden! Aiden, come!" the giant yelled. But he did not follow.

Even with waving the torch back and forth, it could hardly penetrate the darkness. It was too deep, as if it stretched on for eternity. He stepped out further into the cold, dark unknown. If only his father were here.

"You seem to be recovering remarkably," Sir James, Samuel's physician, said. "I can't believe it. I think you may even walk a little sooner than I expected with the help of a crutch."

By the way Alicia had looked at him and giggled, Samuel's face must have lit like a boy who had just been told he was going to a street fair.

"Let me get you a crutch. I'll be right back," James said.

Alicia let out a sigh of relief. "We've been praying for you," she said as she took Samuel by the hand.

Samuel thought it seemed awkward to feel such a gentle, loving touch from someone who belonged to another. Their eyes met.

Alicia's loving expression changed to shame, and she removed her hand from his. "Sorry," Alicia said. "I apparently…"

"No," Samuel said, "that's okay. I understand."

James burst into the room. "Here, this should be about the right size. Do you want to try it now?"

"Sure," Samuel said. He gently leaned forward in his bed, turned ever so slowly, and gingerly planted his feet on the cold, stone floor. He lifted himself up on his left leg as the physician took Samuel's right elbow and helped him to stand. Then Sir James placed a crutch under Samuel's right arm.

"There, how's that?"

As Samuel placed his weight on his leg and crutch, he grimaced. His pride gave him the determination, though, to step forward past the bed.

"Do you think you need two crutches?" the physician asked Samuel.

"Yes," Alicia said. "I think he will."

Slump! Sir Philip dragged the body of Sir Slade from the ravine and laid the drenched cadaver in line with a hundred others.

"Is this the last?" Sir Brendan called out.

"I believe so, Sire," an unidentified voice said. Sir Philip stared at the body of his companion and whispered low, "I don't understand, Lord. But you do. Take his soul and enhance it in your ever-increasing kingdom of power. Here is one more soldier for you. May he join your fight for dominance in the heavenlies and on land."

"Sir Brendan," another unassuming voice called. "We have found another wounded."

"Good," Sir Brendan replied. "Who is he?"

"Sir Jonathan."

Philip spun toward the voice.

"We thought him dead and washed away," the soldier carrying his drenched body said. "But, miraculously, he's alive. I don't understand it. I saw him fall. He should have drowned."

Sir Brendan replied with an unemphatic "Humph," while looking about elsewhere.

Sir Philip walked over. "Yes," Philip said. "I saw him fall, too. You're right. It certainly is a miracle. I'll take him to the recovery center myself if I may?"

"Certainly," Sir Brendan said, straightening himself up a bit. "Many of us will have to carry at least one dead or wounded soldier back with us." His words faded into a mumble.

"What about the king and prince?" the soldier asked. "Who will take them?"

"I will, with a few others," Brendan said. "We will come back for them and bring with us a proper coach in which to return their bodies. I would hate to just have them slumped over a commonlear like the rest of the dead."

"I see," the soldier said.

"Now, let's get these men back home, and quickly," he said. "Who knows if there are any more worgraiths lurking around."

"If there are," Sir Philip added, "they'll probably be here soon. They can smell blood."

"That's right," Sir Brendan said. "Let's not add any more horror to our day."

Aiden inched his way through the darkness. He could feel ravenous eyes staring at him, surrounding him. But was it just his imagination? *They can spot me from anywhere with this torch. But I can't see a thing. I wonder whether it would be worth it to give it up and go alone in the dark.*

The light at least added warmth and comfort. If this was really hell, the damp, cold darkness was unlike what he expected for a place that was supposed to be filled with fire. But the thick, foreboding shadows still presented their own form of torture, a mental torture perhaps equal to that of flames. The loneliness, mixed with the fear of demonic forces leaping out at him from the deep unknown, was torment enough. However, if he's lucky, this wandering alone in the darkness could be the worst of his eternal fate.

Would it have been better to have gone along with the demon? He kept questioning himself. *No, I must keep going. At least I'm free.*

Snap!

Aiden flinched and let out a mild shout.

The giant figure had snapped his fingers and appeared out of thin air just a few steps in front of him, illuminated by a small flame that he held in the palm of his hand.

"Are you ready to come with us yet?" he asked, as if nearly exhausted of all his patience. "Your father is waiting. We have something important to show the both of you. You needn't fear. Come with me."

"My father? You're a liar! My father is not here!"

"Aiden, it's time."

Aiden thought about turning and running but stood frozen.

The being gently reached out his free hand. "Come, and fear not. We have work to do and little time to do it."

"But my father's not here, I know it! I know where I am! I know what you are!"

"Then wander alone in the darkness," the being said. "This is your last chance. Are you coming with us or not?"

Aiden took a defensive stance and eyed this thing closely.

"Aiden, if I were going to attack you, I would have done so by now. Come with me. You're not dead."

"What?" Aiden responded. "Then where am I?"

"Please, come with me. I'll explain everything when we're all together."

"Who's *we*?" Aiden waited for a reply, but the being did not answer. "How do I know you're telling the truth?" Aiden asked. "How do I know you won't lock me in a dungeon or something?"

"Like I said, I would have done so by now. Fear not, for I am an angel of the Lord." The flame in the giant's palm dimmed. "Once this flame is gone, then so will I be gone. You will then be left alone, and you will have to find your own way out. We cannot delay what we have to tell your father any longer."

"How do I know you're telling the truth?"

The flame dimmed further. The blackness enveloped Aiden like a blanket. *Was this being an angel or a deceitful demon in disguise? But he's right. I have no weapon. He could have easily apprehended me— twice, and he hasn't.*

The light in the spirit's palm diminished to nearly nothing. Though he could hardly see the spirit, its eyes pierced Aiden, and he felt from them a sense of trustworthiness. With apprehension in his mind and surrender in his voice, Aiden said, "Okay, I'll go with you."

With Alicia's help, Samuel precariously descended the stairs of the recovery center, but he insisted on hobbling his way out the door on his own.

"Where do you want to go?" she asked once they were outside.

"To the stables."

"Do you think you can walk that far?"

"Yes," Samuel said. His face scrunched "but slowly."

"Okay," she said, brushing her hair from her face. "Why the stables?"

"To pick out my new dragon," he said, flinching as he moved forward a little more.

"Oh," she replied, stepping in line with him. "Do you have one in mind?"

"I do," he said.

"Who?"

"Savannah's son. He's old enough now, and he's trained. Well, at least enough to ride. He'll need a lot of work to get up to speed."

"Does he know—of his mother?" she asked.

"I don't know, but I'm sure someone must have told him."

"Does he have a name?" Alicia asked.

"No. Only masters may name their commonlears. Oh, you received your commonlear at birth like Aiden, didn't you?"

"Yes," she said. "My mother named Autumn Rose, and I think she named Lucinda, too."

"Yes, she did," Samuel said. "I remember that when Aiden and I were quite young, she told the two of us she named both dragons." Samuel wheezed in pain as he proceeded a few more paces. "Aiden never liked the name Lucinda, as I recall. I believe he recently told me he prefers Evelyn Grace. It sounds more royal."

"Oh? When did he say that?"

"Oh, a few weeks ago. We had a break during a training session. Sir Brendan was there, too. And Aric."

A moment of silence passed.

"What are you going to name your new dragon?" Alicia asked quietly.

"Aeric."

What was I thinking to follow this thing…where is he taking me? Can I make it if I run? Should I even try at this point?

Aiden noticed a light up ahead. It was the passageway in the wall—the one Aiden had seen when he first awoke, the passageway where he first encountered this thing.

With his heart beating fast, his legs and arms shaking, Aiden followed the spirit into the first room and then up the stone ramp, down the lighted hallway, and around the corner. His legs almost gave way when he saw a gathering of these beings, and with them, somewhat concealed, was someone else—someone more his size.

He didn't want to make a sudden move. Whether or not this person was a friend or foe, he had to know. Aiden kept his eye on the other creatures as he walked toward the other person. When he got close enough, he peered around these creatures to catch a better glimpse of who or what it was.

"Father, is that you?"

It was just as the spirit promised. He stood among the other beings, who were all dressed similarly, each in a white robe with swords in sheaths, looking like giant living bronze statues sculpted to perfection, with long, flowing hair of all shades.

All had the same blue eyes, each with a fiery glint.

"Aiden!" King Jared yelled as he ran to embrace his son. "I'm so glad you came; why did you run away?"

Aiden backed away.

"Aiden, what's the matter?" King Jared asked.

"He's afraid," the commander said.

"Afraid of what?" King Jared asked.

"Of us," the commander replied. "Of...where he is. He's confused. But—actually, that was all part of the plan."

Aiden twisted his head and furrowed his eyebrows.

"Aiden, I know you think we are demons, but we are not. I know you think you and your father are dead, but you are not. We allowed your commonlears to escape. Letting you escape was too risky—for more reasons than one."

Too perplexed to let out even the slightest sound, Aiden looked at his father, who took hold of both of Aiden's shoulders and looked him squarely in the eye. "Trust them, Aiden. Trust me. This is for real. We are witnessing something that our ancient forefathers long ago had witnessed. And now, for some reason, we have the privilege of being in the company of angels."

"This isn't hell?" Aiden asked, almost childlike.

"No, son, no. You're very much alive. We're still in the cave where we fought the worgraith." King Jared turned toward the commander as the angel approached.

"My name is Xavier," the commanding angel said. "I'm sorry to have not told you at first, but *my* commander told me to allow you to go on like that for a time." Xavier smiled warmly. "Aiden, let me introduce you to my team. This is Tobias, Seth, Sebastian, Nikolas, Timothy, Malachi, Lukas, Kristopher, Titus, Josiah, Dominic, Julian, and Ariel." As Xavier named each angel, they nodded and smiled.

"As we have been explaining to your father, we have been on a critical operation here, and Our Lord would like us to reveal it to you in this manner. Like your father said, this kind of angelic visitation hasn't happened in millennia, and we don't know if or when we will ever do this again. Actually, it's quite a delight to reveal ourselves to humans again."

"The idea you had about baiting the worgraith and getting it to chase your crew," Lukas added, "we planted that idea in your mind, Aiden, and we made sure that you and your father were caught so that you were separated from your troop."

"But why?" Aiden asked.

"So, our enemies could think that they had won, that you were dead and out of the way," Xavier explained. "Now, they have no idea you're alive and with us. So, they cannot try to intervene with any plans we may make, and they will certainly not know that we are about to show you their greatest secret."

A wintry chill greeted the juvenile commonlears as Alicia opened the stable doors.

"A young lady should not have to do such a chivalrous task for…"

"You are in no condition to open the door for me or for yourself. I have opened this door a thousand times before. I can do it again."

Samuel grunted a 'thank you' and hobbled past her as quickly as he could. Alicia followed behind for a moment, concealing her quiet laughter at his masculine pride. The stalls were unusually quiet.

"There you are," Samuel said. The somewhat small, black commonlear had a hint of purple that shone when the light hit his scales just right. His expression revealed a shattered and hopeless heart. His body shook and cowered. This was, without a doubt, the loneliest and most pitiful commonlear Samuel had ever seen.

"Oh," Alicia said. "The poor thing looks devastated."

"Losing your mother is devastating," Samuel added. "I know what it's like. We both do, don't we?" he said, turning to Alicia.

"Now all three of us do," she said.

A moment of silence crept by as they both tried to find something to say that could bring some hope to the young dragon.

"Hey there," Samuel began. "You're seven years old now," he said. "You're old enough to be ridden. How would you like to be mine?"

The small dragon's eyes lit up a little as he nodded.

"You would?"

He nodded again.

"Can I call you Aeric?"

The commonlear seemed to think for a moment, and then in a sort of a far-off way, as if still pondering, not sure what to think, nodded.

"Great. This is Alicia. Can you say hi?"

The commonlear got up from the corner of his pen and walked over to greet Alicia.

"Oh," she said. "He's so sweet." She held out her hand, and he sniffed for a moment as he put his nose in her palm.

"He likes you," Samuel said as he watched the wonderful way in which she warmly engaged this frightened young creature. They heard a loud whooshing sound from above.

"It's the knights," they said in unison.

Jeff Miller

Ten

The band of angels led Aiden and King Jared down the corridor. The ground was a little slippery in places, like walking a stone pathway after a light rain. A light mist in the cold air almost clung to Aiden's face. The sound of dripping water reverberated from somewhere in the distance. A dimly lit doorway was just ahead. They halted.

Xavier turned around and gazed directly into Aiden's eyes. "Gentlemen," he whispered, "come forward."

The angels moved aside to allow Aiden and his father room to walk. When they were close enough, Xavier continued in a hush. "What I am about to show you is our discovery. Our men have been trying to track this demonic force for a long time. But the demons have been evading us, keeping just one step ahead. When you three squires were attacked, Aiden, we finally knew where to search—here, in Whiterock. With help from our spies, we followed the worgraith to his lair in this cave. Then, upon further investigation, our spies found this room. They came across it just yesterday. Actually, Aeric was very helpful with our search. Are you ready?"

The king nodded. Aiden was stunned. *What did he mean, 'Aeric was very helpful'?*

"Stay close," Xavier whispered. "I have felt their presence for some time now. They're definitely there." He walked quietly just a few steps further then stopped, listened, and turned to look at his men. Xavier nodded, and then he and his troops quietly unsheathed their swords.

"Your Majesty," Xavier whispered. "I'm afraid you must excuse us. This will only take but a moment. Stay here." Xavier and his angels snuck up to the doorway.

Aiden backed away. He sensed horrific evil emanating from that room. It felt like death. It crept through his spirit and down his spine like a slithery snake. Aiden focused on Xavier. The angelic commander's eyes were on something, or someone, moving in the darkness. Whatever it was, it was likely the source of this permeating evil.

Xavier kept quiet. Then, like a hunter tracking his prey, Xavier lifted his sword, halted, and let out a loud, frightening scream of vengeance. He hurled into the darkness in a swift flash of light. The other angels followed in the same swift, lightning-like manner, leaving Aiden and his father alone in utter darkness, listening to the screams and cries of warriors in the shadows.

As swords clashed, angels and other beings moaned and wailed, some in thunderous warlike authority, some in wild animal-like growls and roars, others in screams of agony. These sounds of terror pierced Aiden's ears. He had never heard anything quite like it before.

King Jared's expression turned from fear to faith. He moved toward the door to see what was going on.

"What do you see?" Aiden asked. "Do you see anything?"

"I see flashes of light," King Jared replied. "And in differing degrees. It looks like quick bursts like lightning and smoke as swords clash with each other—in other cases, as the swords are moving through the air, it seems as if their swords are sometimes reflecting light. Reflecting from what or where, I don't know."

Aiden drew near to his father as they both watched what was happening in the darkness with amazement. It looked as if angels were fighting angels.

King Jared slowly looked away from the battle to Aiden. The king's eyes widened as his mouth opened in thought. "This is it," he said. "This is the sound I heard in the cave just before we split from Sir Brendan, the sound of men and swords clashing. Aiden, it was the angels fighting demons somewhere in the cave before we arrived."

A high-pitched, menacing roar blasted from behind Aiden and King Jared. They both jumped in fear at the sudden, dreadful sound. The being's dull glow was barely enough for Aiden to make out its features. From what Aiden could see, it was certainly as huge and mighty as an angel. It stared at him with fury and anticipation, like it had waited for this moment for a long time.

Face contorted and hair disheveled, Aiden could tell the being had once been something majestic, but its once pristine robes had become tattered and dirty, and its eyes blazed with a different sort of fire. This apparently evil angel still had its bronze skin, but as with aged and unpolished bronze, its skin had become marred and discolored. The evil being raised its sword, eager and ready to strike. Aiden looked over at his father, who also watched this thing, powerless.

"King!" Xavier bellowed from the darkness, still fighting. "He is not flesh and bone. Physical swords won't work against spirits, and his sword won't work against you. I mean, it can, to a degree— it can unleash demonic power into your soul. I think it wants to unleash something into Aiden's soul. You must use your authority to prevent him from doing this—not your earthly authority as King, but your heavenly authority as a child of God."

The demon acted as if it would strike at any moment.

"I think it's hesitating because of our presence. You might have time. Cast it away, quick! With your words! Cast out all demonic power already oppressing Aiden! King Jared, you have the power of God within you! Do not permit it to unleash power into…" Xavier's words cut short as another attacker came upon him quickly.

With what seemed to be a sudden newfound sense of courage and understanding, King Jared extended his finger at the beast. "You cannot harm my son! You cannot enter into and oppress him! Leave him alone, you and all your wretched ilk." Then King Jared turned to Aiden and put his hand on his shoulder. "That which is already oppressing him, begone!" The demon seemed stunned as it stared at what looked like shadows lifting from Aiden's soul. Aiden felt his spirit lighten.

Gathering fury, the demon lifted its sword. Aiden and his father both flinched, but the demon's sword stopped in mid swing, as if hitting an unseen barrier. It tried to strike again, and still it couldn't. The demon's eyes widened. It tried to leap toward Aiden but jerked back as if restrained by a leash.

"You shall not have my son!" the king commanded.

The demon screamed as a swirl of wind and fire enclosed it. Its sword fell from its hand. Then, out of nowhere, braces and chains bound the demon. Then the swirl of wind and fire fully enveloped the demon, and the evil being vanished from their sight.

A blinding light instantly overcame the darkness behind them. Aiden and King Jared shielded their eyes as they turned. Xavier shouted, "See, we are overcoming your darkness—we are weakening your power! Now, I proclaim by the authority of God, go—all of you wretched rebels, into the fire, into the pit! Leave the Kingdom of Whiterock and never return!"

A wild wind replaced the sound of colliding swords. Underneath that, Aiden could faintly hear the sounds of chains, locks. The demons screamed. In a moment, all was silent. The light softened and was no longer blinding.

An almost deafening hush fell over the cave as if nothing had happened. The only thing Aiden could hear was the pounding of his own heart. He trembled. The angels illuminated the room with their very beings so he and his father could see. It was what seemed to be a typical grotto but with papers and bound books all around; some on tables, and some on elaborate stands. There were candle stands, too. Crude benches faced what seemed to be a platform in a rough, natural cavity in the wall.

The platform consisted of a lectern, candle stands, and some kind of table. An elaborately carved throne made from marble sat on a slightly elevated platform behind the table.

"Come," Xavier said. He gestured for the king and prince of Whiterock to enter. "You need to see this more closely."

Alicia again opened the stable doors for Samuel as he hobbled as quickly as he could. This time, he was in too much of a hurry, too much of a worry, to care about his pride.

They walked a few steps and looked up. Their eyes stung from the sunlight bursting through the dark clouds. Alicia held her hand to her brow to shield the sun.

"Do you see father or Aiden?" she asked Samuel as a cold burst of wild wind whipped through the courtyard.

"No, not yet," he said. "They've got to be here somewhere. Maybe they landed already. Maybe they're conversing with Lord Donovan."

"That could be," Alicia said. "They've probably landed on the other side, or maybe on my father's balcony. It's large enough for two commonlears."

As she continued to scour the area for her father and brother, her eyes landed on Sir Philip. He was carrying Sir Jonathan in both arms, face contorted as he staggered.

"*Philip!*" she cried.

Alicia took a step forward and then hesitated. She nearly started again but held herself back. "I'm so glad Philip is alive," she said. "But…he needs to tend to Sir Jonathan." She looked around. Her voice quaked. "There are so many dead and wounded." Tears welled in her eyes. "I still don't see them."

"Don't worry. They're fine," Samuel said, his voice unsure.

But those words had barely left his lips when she saw Sir Brendan coming directly toward her from seemingly out of nowhere. Once her eyes met his, he tilted his face to the ground. He walked more slowly than normal. His once proud posture had collapsed. A few times, his feet scuffed the earth. Sir Brendan bowed to the princess on one knee, still looking to the ground. His voice quivered. "My Lady, it is with deep sorrow that I must inform you that your father and brother fought bravely together to destroy the enemy."

Alicia knew what he was about to say next. It could only be one thing. She covered her mouth as tears streamed down her face.

"I am truly sorry," Sir Brendan said as another icy wind buffeted the forlorn threesome.

Alicia looked desperately at Samuel, who could only stare back in disbelief.

"They were heroes," Sir Brendan said. Gaining his composure and lifting his head, he looked her in the eye. "If it were not for them, many of us would have died at the hands of a worgraith. They distracted it so we could regroup and lead it into a trap."

Alicia glanced quickly again at Samuel, and without a word, she ran off to the recovery center.

As Sir Brendan's eyes followed Alicia, Samuel noticed those eyes seemed to dim, almost looking past Alicia in a blank, unfocused gaze.

"They were good friends, both of them," Sir Brendan said. He looked at Samuel and stood.

Samuel winced as he asked, "And their bodies?"

"Still in a cave behind High Falls," Sir Brendan said. "We'll be sending out a party to retrieve them. I did not want them to come home like this. They deserve to be brought home separately, in a royal hearse, with a ceremony."

"You're right," Samuel agreed, bowing his head. "What about the worgraiths?"

"We killed three altogether, but there might be more. We don't know," Sir Brendan admitted. "I see you're doing much better, thank God."

"Yeah," he said as he looked around, his blood beginning to boil.

Squires ran and called for their masters, wounded were hauled into the recovery center, and young dead soldiers were being lined up on the ground. There was panic in everyone's eyes, and shouts for help still sounded in all directions. Nurses were told to go back inside, tend to the wounded there, and help keep things in order.

Squires sprawled all over the castle grounds, treating their master's lesioned steeds with ointments and spirits and bandages. Some blood-soaked dragons had to be held down with ropes by several squires as the dragons' gashes were stitched. But the steeds seemed to not be in as dire of a condition as their masters—many wounded commonlears had died either during battle or shortly thereafter and remained where they fell.

"Thank *God*," Samuel said sarcastically. "Thank God all you want for this."

Samuel turned and hobbled on his crutches back toward Aeric's stable. Sir Brendan watched him go then turned toward the castle. His eyes caught Lord Donovan's, who was near the recovery center steps. The one in charge of the entire kingdom seemed just as lost as everyone else. Maybe more so, for although he was a noble, he did not seem to have the right skills to lend a hand.

Lord Donovan's eyes caught Sir Brendan's. The lord rushed to him, asked, "Where are they? Where's my son?"

Sir Brendan bowed his head a little as he looked into Lord Donovan's eyes. "Your son is fine," he answered. "He's here somewhere."

"Sir Jonathan, my nephew? Is he alright?"

"It's hard to say, Sire."

"And the king and prince?" he asked.

Sir Brendan hesitated, averting his gaze, and held his breath. It must have answered the question well enough, for Lord Donovan's eyes widened with grief as he clenched both hands and pounded them into Sir Brendan's chest armor. Bowing his head, he burst into tears. The lord then turned and walked off into the distance, head still bowed, wailing for his fallen king and prince.

Alicia hurried through the recovery center in tears.

"Princess! Why are you here? What do you need? Can I help, your majesty?"

"Oh, Brianna!" Alicia said as she turned to the voice. "I'm so glad to see you!"

Brianna had been one of several women who regularly took Alicia under her wing after her mother died—at the request of

King Jared—giving her a proper education and teaching her how to be a princess and a Godly woman.

"Philip, he's here somewhere. Please, help me find Philip."

"I'll stay with you," Brianna said.

"Thank you," Alicia answered.

"I have not seen him on this floor, but please, your highness, come with me. Maybe they will know upstairs."

Brianna walked with her from one station to the next, describing both Philip and Jonathan and asking if anyone had seen them. After three more flights, a nurse said that she had seen them and that she thought he was somewhere in station two or three— where the women had previously looked—but the nurse wasn't sure exactly which one or if he was in either of those stations anymore for sure.

"The fifth and sixth floors are full," she said. "I'm pretty sure he is not up there. They started filling those floors first, since they were hardly occupied. But I think he was one of the last to come in."

"He was," Alicia said. "I saw him walk in. He was one of the last."

"Thank you," Brianna said to the nurse. "We'll go back down. We'll start with the fourth floor. Thank you, again."

The two backtracked. The disorder on the fourth floor seemed to settle. A physician noticed Alicia and Brianna. "Your highness," he said with a bow. "The man you were looking for, he's here. Down the hallway at the very last room."

"Thank you," Brianna said. Alicia took her hand. Brianna led her down the hallway.

Alicia's entire body had wilted. She sighed deeply and hardly found the strength to hold her head high again. Alicia involuntarily held her breath as they approached the room.

Her footsteps grabbed Philip's attention. He spun around, and before he had recognized her, Alica embraced Philip with such force that he stumbled back slightly.

"I can't believe what I see," King Jared said. "What is this? It looks like a temple."

"That's exactly what it is, Your Majesty," Xavier answered.

"But a temple for what?" Aiden asked. "For whom?"

Xavier nodded to Lukas, who held a large, leather-bound book. "In all the kingdoms established since the dawn of time, we have been expecting something like this to arise eventually." Xavier said. "Apparently, Lucifer decided that this was the time and place. In answer to your questions," Xavier took the book from Lukas and handed it to King Jared. "I think this says it all."

"Hope, Revolution, and Despair," King Jared read aloud.

Aiden stood so close to his father that they touched shoulders. The two slowly perused the book. Some angels disappeared for reasons unsaid. The Heavenly warriors who remained walked up to torches around the walls and lit them with a simple wave of hand.

Aiden turned his attention from the angels to the book in his father's hands. He noticed that the brown-red leather cover had the title written in an intricate gold lettering with a beautiful thin-lined gold arrangement bordering the cover. Inside were thick yellow-brown pages with elaborate handwriting. "Father, what type of paper is that? Have you seen anything like that before?"

"No, son, I haven't."

"You wouldn't have," Xavier explained. "It's not of this world. Nor is the ink, for that matter. It's a spiritual compound Satan conjured into physical."

"Really?" King Jared asked. "Can this be done?"

"It can," Xavier answered. "But it is forbidden. However, Lucifer sometimes does what he wants, regardless."

"Sometimes?" King Jared asked.

"Sometimes," Xavier answered.

King Jared turned some pages and read aloud the contents. "*The Eternal Beginning; The Creation of the Heavens; The Time of Ourselves; The Turning; Revolution*…What is this?" King Jared asked.

"It's Lucifer's personal memoir of his rebellion."

"*The* rebellion? From Lucifer's perspective?" the king asked.

"Yes. It's generally true, to a degree," Xavier answered. "The facts are mostly accurate, but again, it's all from his perspective. It doesn't delve into just how defiant and power-hungry Lucifer is. It's written as if he and his angels are the heroes, as if God were a cruel and evil king, one from whom they had to declare their independence to begin a new, better, freer kingdom."

Xavier stopped speaking and stared into space, deep in thought—deep in memory. Then he began again, "Satan and his demons actually believe everything that's written there. But they have such a skewed perspective on our God. I remember before the fall, our side tried to explain it all to them. How they were wrong, how they just didn't understand."

He paused again. "But it was no use. Their anger and bitterness—their pride and arrogance—just got in the way of listening. They thought their ways were better, fairer. And as I said, they revolted against Him and against us. And now, it's war. There is no turning back."

"War?" Aiden asked. "War over what?"

"The souls of men. The order of the universe," Xavier said. "When God deems the war over, it will be over. But until He squashes Satan for good—until all have had a chance at redemption before the realm of time ends—we have battles to fight. And so do you."

Aiden was silent for a moment. "So, what does this book have to do with all this?" He peered around the room.

Xavier nodded to Josiah, who brought over another book and handed it to Aiden. This book was bound in black and had gold lettering designed similarly to the first one.

"*The Power Within,*" Aiden read aloud. "What is this?"

"This book has to do with all that you see around you," Xavier explained. "It is this cult's holy scriptures written by Lucifer himself."

Aiden slowly, almost hesitantly, opened the book. In it, he saw what appeared to be hand-written instructions. "Are these…is this Satan's own handwriting?" Aiden asked.

"It is," Xavier explained. "I'd know that handwriting anywhere."

"It's beautiful," King Jared noticed.

"I can't believe this," Aiden said, his eyes fixated on the pages. "It's all about how majestic and loving and kind and wonderful Lucifer is; how evil God is; how evil and full of deceit the followers of God are."

Aiden looked over the pages some more, stricken with terror as his eyes beheld words he could not bear to see. His hands started shaking, and his eyes could not leave the page.

King Jared read the chapter title aloud, "*Sickness, Disease, and Death: Jehovah's Plan for Cruelty to Humankind.* Aiden, what's the matter?"

Aiden did not answer but handed the book to his father. He felt dizzy and sick to his stomach thinking about his mother, about Aeric.

King Jared continued turning the pages and reading the chapter titles. The more he read, the more he understood how this book became scripture for a religious cult. "Lucifer, the Bright, and Morning Star," Then he read another chapter name, "Entering the Presence of Almighty Lucifer," and, "Listening to His Voice." Then he skipped to the final chapter headings, "Revenge and Control," and finally, "Rewards in Hell."

"Those last two," Xavier said, "are the most dangerous and have motivated the most recent plans for this cult, some of which have already begun, and the rest, if we don't act quickly, will happen at any time."

"What do you mean?" King Jared asked.

Xavier nodded toward Titus, who handed the king a scroll from one of the pedestals. The king opened it, and after a moment, he slowly sat down on a bench, his mouth agape and his eyes glazed in deep thought.

"What is it?" Aiden asked.

King Jared opened the scroll slightly and read the heading to his son. "The Plan to Control Whiterock." King Jared read the rest slowly.

Alicia felt comfort in Philip's arms. She knew that without him, she would have nothing. The two walked from the recovery center outside, where they could get some fresh air and, hopefully, some peace. The hustle and bustle settled down. Many knights had by now gone to their encampments to rest, mourn, gather their thoughts, and wait for further instruction. Other knights were finishing making rounds to encampments, telling unfortunate squires the news that they would never again see their beloved knights.

The air was getting colder, and the sky grew darker. Alicia shivered. "Here, let me put this on you," Philip said. "It'll help." He took off a cape and placed it around Alicia. The two walked toward the stables, and as they did, Sir Brendan approached.

"Sir Philip," he said in a commanding tone, "may I have a brief word with you?"

Sir Philip looked at Alicia. "I'll be but a moment." She smiled in affirmation as Philip and Sir Brendan walked just out of earshot.

"Sir Philip, as you know, we are forming a party to retrieve the king and his son and bring their bodies back in a royal coach. I would like you to assist, and I'll need men to go in case we find another worgraith. I know this is short notice, but I believe we should do this as quickly as possible. Are you willing to round up some troops?"

"I am always willing to assist," Sir Philip said. "I'm honored to help you lead this next mission."

"Good."

"Sir," Philip whispered, "what about the crowning ceremony? I think the crowning ceremony would be a good time to announce our betrothal publicly."

Sir Brendan's eyes burned into Philip's. He took a breath and said, "I must confer with Zachariah and your father."

"Oh, yes," Philip replied, "of course."

Then Sir Brendan asked, nodding slightly in Alicia's direction, "How is she?"

"She needs comfort. I think I should spend some time with her."

Sir Brendan nodded. "Not long. We have work to do." He left the two alone.

"So, they bred these worgraiths?" Aiden asked. "It was all part of a plan to kill us?"

"Yes," Xavier said.

King Jared added, "And so long as the members had protection from Satan and his demons, they could not be killed?"

"Yes," Xavier said. "That is, until *we* came along. We sort of ruined thier plans."

"How do you mean?" Aiden asked.

"We started fighting the demons, much like you saw us do here, but alongside you and your knights. We were invisible to you. Some of The Power Within, as they call themselves, ended up losing their covering, thanks to us."

"So, you're privy to who's part of this cult?" King Jared asked.

"Oh, yes. Absolutely," Xavier answered.

"Then, who are they?" King Jared asked.

Xavier walked to a scroll that was on another pedestal, took it, and handed it to King Jared. "Here are all the names of the cult members, as far as we know."

"Samuel? Is that you? Are you still here?"

The young man looked up from his position, sitting inside Aeric's stall. When he turned to face the sweet voice that called his name, he noticed she wasn't alone; Philip accompanied her. The glimmer of hope he felt at hearing Alicia's voice again turned to embarrassment as he realized she and Philip found him crouched in hay inside his commonlear's stall.

"Oh, yes," he replied, trying not to let his combined embarrassment and sudden broken heart show. "I wanted to get away from the crowd, the noise, the confusion. Besides, I thought I should get to know Aeric."

"Aeric? You named your new commonlear Aeric?" Sir Philip asked. "That's…that's nice."

Pleasantly surprised at Philip's kindness, Samuel replied, "Thank you. He's Savannah's son. I picked him out today." He winced as he clung to a beam in the stall and eased himself to standing.

"Oh, please, let me help you," Alicia held out her hand.

"*Alicia*," Philip quietly scolded.

But she ignored him and brushed the hay off of Samuel, who felt even more embarrassed that someone else's fiancé had her hands on him, and it was evident from Philip's intense, burning stare that he didn't like it at all.

"I should be going," Samuel said. "I shouldn't be away from the recovery center too much longer. They'll come looking for me."

"I don't think you have to worry about that," Alicia replied. "I think they have their hands full."

Samuel kept his gaze on Philip's glaring scowl, burning with hatred toward him. This fueled a fire in Samuel. If Alicia weren't there, and if he were in a better fighting condition, he would confront Philip's anger. But he thought it was best to leave before he made a rash decision that he would later regret. Alicia opened the stall door, and Samuel hobbled out without a word.

Once Samuel was out of earshot, Philip said in a quiet anger, "What were you doing? You are engaged to me, not him!"

"Philip, what do you mean? What was I doing?'"

"You are a lady of nobility who is engaged to a man of nobility, and you had your hands on him!"

"Philip, he's my friend. He's like a brother. Besides, he *is* nobility. His grandfather will be crowned king, he will be the new…" Alicia's face contorted, her eyes welling with tears as she remembered that she no longer had a family. She looked down, hiding her tears. "Samuel is on crutches," she squeaked. "He just needed some help standing; that's all."

He took a step closer. She looked into his eyes. Instead of seeing compassion for Samuel's condition and for the tragic loss of her father and brother, she only saw a fury in him that surpassed any she had seen before. Her mind numbed as her body froze with fear, stealing her breath.

"You will let him get up on his own; and if he can't, you just let him stay." Stepping even closer to her and pointing his finger in her face, Philip commanded, "I don't ever want to see you touch another man again; do you understand?"

Alicia took a breath and swallowed. *Perhaps I had gone too far*, she thought. *I didn't know. I was just trying to help.* She wanted to get those words out and apologize for her ignorance, but she couldn't. After a moment, Alicia found enough strength to whisper, voice shaking as a tear rolled down her face, "I understand."

"*Philip?*" King Jared cried as he read the scroll. "Xavier, this is the man betrothed to my daughter!"

"I knew it!" Aiden added. "Somehow, all I could think of was Philip when I saw all of this. Father, I tried to tell you. There's something about him…"

"He may be the cult's leader, but we're not sure," Xavier said. "There's more,"

"More?" King Jared asked.

"We've found another scroll."

Xavier, now the only angel left in the room, took one small scroll from the podium. He handed it to King Jared.

The king opened it as Aiden peered over his shoulder. In a wild, beastly style that looked like it had been written in blood with careless drips and splatters, the king and his son made out the words:

ALICIA -> SACRIFICE, CONSECRATE CASTLE

Aiden and King Jared looked at one another and then silently followed Xavier to the platform. He showed them the table that sat between the podium and the throne. On it were small bones, bloodstains, and fur.

"As you can see, there is evidence here of animal sacrifices," Xavier said. "But, Your Majesty, if that note is any warning, your daughter may be next—their first human sacrifice—and it will happen inside the castle."

"Dear God," King Jared gasped, "we have to get back to the castle as soon as possible! And is that Philip's throne?"

"No," Xavier replied. "That is where Satan sits."

Shock flowed through King Jared. His mind spun. His stomach churned. He could hardly raise his voice above a whisper. "Why would anyone so intently invite Satan…how could anyone…" the king choked and tried again. "How could anyone, let alone my own men whom I've known and trusted, be so…*so evil?* How did this happen…and why?"

"Trust me," Xavier said softly. "There are many of us still asking that same question of our once beloved brother and his followers."

King Jared cleared his throat and looked back at the empty chair. He wanted so badly for Satan to appear—just so he could look straight in his wretched, haughty face. The king's heart raced, and his whole being shook. He inched closer to the throne, his legs a bit wobbly. He pointed his shaky finger at the empty chair. His voice quivered at first and finally erupted into a mighty roar. "You shall not take my daughter! You shall not take my kingdom! We are on the side of God Almighty! And we shall win!"

TWELVE

Samuel hobbled up the stairs that led to his room. Although it seemed as if all had settled down, so much had happened in such a short amount of time.

He opened the door. Someone had taken his bed. Letting out a loud sigh mixed with a snarl, Samuel angrily searched for the nearest nurse. "Excuse me, what's going on here? Someone is in my bed."

"We thought you left," the nurse replied.

"No," Samuel answered. "I just went out for a walk."

The nurse rolled her eyes and sighed. "I'll find the physician."

Samuel let out his own loud sigh of frustration as he followed her out the door and into the hallway. Sir James was right there.

"This young man says his bed is taken," the nurse snapped.

"Ah, yes. I couldn't find you," Sir James began. "You seem to be doing much better, so we're releasing you."

"You're releasing me? Why didn't you say anything?"

"I just did."

"I mean before."

"You weren't around. How could we have said anything? And with the others coming in so fast, we had to find room wherever we could." Sir James waved his hand around. "These knights, they are in much dire need. And we had to use your bed. I'm sure you'll be fine. There's nothing more we can do. You've been recuperating amazingly well."

Samuel sighed again, looked down to the floor, and said, "Can someone at least help me back down the stairs and out the door?"

"Of course we can," said Sir James. "Nurse, help this young man back down the stairs and out the door."

Silence fell over the grotto. Aiden walked away from the front of the temple, where his father stayed to examine more documents. Xavier stayed with him. As the king searched through additional books that were apparently written in Satan's own handwriting, he and Xavier discussed what they found—many spells, charms, and potions that included how to make a princess fall in love, how to conjure protection, and how to be victorious in just about anything. King Jared even found books that told secrets of where to find and what spells to use to capture and breed worgraiths.

Some scrolls delved into a complex series of underground networks of secret dragon breeders located all over the world. One in particular, "Sands of the South," was circled. "These secret merchants—mostly wizards and warlocks—buy and sell all kinds of dragons bred for destruction. Hopefully, worgraiths are the only breed of these nefarious dragons in Whiterock," Xavier said.

Aiden walked toward the back of the grotto temple, trying to let it all sink in. *Good, evil, God, Satan—what was going on? Is God good after all? Or is Satan's perception of Heaven's history right? No, not if Satan commanded Alicia to be killed, not if he commanded the worgraiths to destroy Whiterock. Not if Satan's worgraiths killed Aeric.*

Breathless, Aiden's eyes widened. *Philip killed Aeric. Philip's men were to blame for all the slaughtered knights—not God. It is Satan that is to blame for all of this. God is on the side of the kingdom. The angels' intervention proves it—Xavier saved me from that horrific demon trying to enter something into my soul. But still—why would an all-powerful God even allow such a thing?*

Aiden walked some more along the back wall near a tapestry. The black tapestry depicted a golden goat's head inside a star that was inside a gold circle. While still deep in thought, Aiden hardly noticed his arm unintentionally brushing against it. He certainly didn't notice the way it stirred, the way the goat's head looked down on him, as if he had just awoken it.

Aiden turned to his father. "What about Lord Donovan?" he asked. "He must be part of this if his son and all of his men are involved. Lord Donovan has become the steward of all of Whiterock. He must be the mastermind behind all of this. But then, Zachariah would be crowned king, wouldn't he?"

"Zachariah would be placed as king, yes," King Jared said. "As much as it pains me, Aiden, that thought about Lord Donovan has come to my mind." King Jared took a step toward Aiden. "But I can't imagine…of course, I never would have imagined *any* of this. But I don't see his name on any of the ledgers. It all seems to indicate Philip is in charge."

"We don't know if these ledgers are all-inclusive," Xavier said, slowly closing the book in his hands. "We only found these yesterday. I've told you everything I know up to this point. His name could be intentionally kept out of this, as an alibi, just in case it's found."

"You're right," King Jared said. "After all, it was he who suggested that Aiden come along with us on this mission. Maybe he wanted to make sure the both of us died together—to get us out of the way."

"We can't afford to be wrong," Xavier said. "We must discover whether Lord Donovan is part of this." Xavier set the book down.

"But why would Lord Donovan keep quiet?" Aiden asked. "If he were part of this, then why wouldn't his name be on anything? Wouldn't he want all the glory? It looks as if Philip is getting all the fame here."

King Jared stroked his beard. "Lord Donovan may want to remain anonymous if he's to have the throne. But then, if his plan fails, he risks losing his only son by letting him take the blame for everything. Insurgence is punishable by death. And what would Philip have to gain by agreeing to that? So, it's more probable that Lord Donovan isn't a part of this ring."

"It sounds like a counterfeit of God's plan of redemption for you," Xavier said. "In order to win mankind back from Satan's grasp, God's Son willingly sacrificed Himself. He did it out of obedience to His Father—out of His love for Him."

"Is that what this is all about?" King Jared chimed. "Is Philip willing to sacrifice himself for his father's obsession with my throne? That doesn't make sense."

"That's true," Xavier answered. "God the Father loved mankind so much that He bought you at the highest price He could—the life of His only Son—to redeem you back to Him. Philip sacrificing himself for his father's obsession doesn't sound as worthy of a plan, but with Satan, motives are usually selfish. Maybe part of the counterfeit strategy is that Satan swore an oath to raise Philip from the dead," Xavier continued. "Then they'd have a false Messiah for their cult."

"Could Satan be trusted to honor an oath?" King Jared asked.

"It's possible if the promise benefitted him in the long run." Xavier began pacing. "Philip has a hunger for power. Satan, I'm sure, has promised him this—somehow, somewhere, someway. Perhaps in death. But again, we're assuming too much…"

"Then I suppose there is only one way to find out whether Lord Donovan is part of all this," King Jared said. "I must confront him. And I pray that we're wrong."

As Aiden soaked all of this in, he leaned back against the black tapestry. When he did, the wall moved. He fell back, ripping the tapestry down with him.

"Aiden!" his father cried.

Samuel fought against the powerful wind that pushed against the recovery center's doors. The weather had changed drastically in just that day, and the cold wind slammed into him so hard it hurt.

Shivering, Samuel made his way on his crutches to the stables to get Aeric. Samuel did not have a saddle or bridle for Aeric yet, which meant he would have to ride him bareback—an unpleasant thought, considering Samuel's current physical condition. Samuel opened the stable doors and walked to Aeric's stall. As he drew closer, Samuel could hear a faint weeping.

"Hello?" Samuel said, his eyes trying to adjust to the darkness. "Are you alright? Who is it?" Sitting hunched over, crying, just outside Aeric's stall was the figure of a young lady. "Alicia, is that you?"

She turned. "Oh, Samuel. I wished you hadn't seen me like this," she said, wiping her tears.

"This stall must be cursed," Samuel said in a feeble attempt to cheer Alicia. "It seems this is the third time today someone's sat here mourning."

She didn't respond.

"Alicia, I'm sorry. I know how much it must hurt to have lost your entire family. I don't know what to say."

"And there's more," she said. "Philip. Something's gotten into him. I've never seen him act this way. He had an anger that was just…indescribable." She looked up at Samuel. "It was you. He went stark-raving mad over the way I tried to help you. I didn't know what else to do." Alicia sighed.

Samuel grimaced and groaned as he gingerly sat down next to her. Aeric brushed his nose through the wooden beams and wagged his tail. As Alicia felt Aeric's nose nudge between her and Samuel, she smiled.

"Hey," Samuel said. "What are you trying to do, huh? I think he wants to cheer you up, Alicia."

"I think he already did," Alicia said as she petted Aeric on the nose, who then backed away into his stall.

Samuel inched closer to Alicia. He so desperately wanted to lean his shoulder against hers, but he knew he couldn't.

"Maybe it's the battle," she said. "Maybe it had gotten to him." Alicia's voice weakened. "And after losing my father and brother. Oh, Samuel." Then her tears fell, but for only a moment. She placed her forehead on Samuel's shoulder. A moment passed, and her tears subsided. Alicia then looked up at Samuel with eyes full of confusion and sorrow. She sat up and inched away from him.

Neither noticed the figure observing them. Philip's eyes burned with a demonic hatred as he clenched his teeth and squeezed his fists tightly. But he left the stables quietly enough that neither Alicia nor Samuel heard.

Alicia rose to her feet, turned, and stumbled away.

"Alicia, please. Are you alright?" Samuel asked.

She did not answer. "Ow!" Samuel winced as he grabbed the stall beams to stand. As she made her way toward the door, she held her hand up, indicating she did not want to be near him now. "Please…Alicia!"

Aiden landed hard at the bottom of a series of carved steps. He grunted as he slowly sat up and placed his hand on his back.

"Aiden! Are you alright?"

"I'm fine, father," he said, his discomfort evident in his voice. "I'm down here."

Aiden noticed a light penetrating the darkness as he looked behind him and heard the footsteps of his father and Xavier resounding down the stairs. As Xavier and King Jared came closer, the glory emanating from the angel unveiled another grotto. This one, however, was much larger.

"What is this?" King Jared asked.

"Look," Xavier said, pointing. "There, at the end."

Aiden got up and followed his father and the angel.

"I don't believe it," King Jared said.

The end of the tunnel sparkled and shimmered—gold, ruby, and emerald.

As they reached the pile of treasure, King Jared said, "This is ours. This is our treasure—the treasure of Whiterock—the treasure of my forefathers. It's just a small portion, but how did it get here? And when? No one but Zachariah and I know where…"

The king froze, dazed, as he stared at the pile. "That means… Zachariah," he whispered brokenly, "…oh no, could *he* be one of them?"

Jeff Miller

THIRTEEN

Steps echoed through a long, dark, arched stone hallway deep within the recesses of the castle.

"My Lord," Zachariah began. "The greatest treasure known to man has been Whiterock's greatest secret for generations. As king, you will be its steward."

The three stopped at the end of the tunnel. Zachariah gently brushed his hand across the wall, trying to find the marker. There it was: a small knob.

"Take one of the nearby torches," Zachariah said as he grabbed one for himself. "You'll need it." Zachariah placed his hand back on the marker and twisted. It clicked and clacked several times.

"Dear Zachariah," Lord Donovan said. "I wish you would reconsider your decision. The people trust your leadership. You have been at King Jared's side for years; he would have wanted you to be the rightful heir."

"No, I believe this arrangement would be best," Zachariah said. "Besides, Philip is engaged to the princess; it only seems right to keep the kingdom in the royal bloodline. No, I believe the Lord above has other plans for me. I can't explain it, and I don't know what it is yet, but…" he turned his ear. "Brace yourself; it should start any moment now."

Sounds of soft rumbles and scrapes penetrated through the wall. Lord Donovan and Sir Philip stumbled slightly as the floor beneath them sank. Their eyes widened in astonishment. Philip smiled as the floor descended into a dark shaft. There, by the light of the torches, the three faced an iron door. Zachariah took his lamp and placed it near the door's lock. From a bag slung around his torso, Zachariah produced a tiny iron dagger with a chiseled engraving on its point. He slid the dagger into the lock and twisted.

The sound of three large bolts unlocking echoed loudly in the shallow hall. With all his might, Zachariah pushed on the door, but it wouldn't budge. "Can you help me?" he asked.

The father and son set down their torches and joined Zachariah in slamming their shoulders against the iron door. It did nothing. They all looked at each other then heaved again. It budged a little. The three heaved once more. It opened.

After lifting their torches and taking a moment for their eyes to adjust, Zachariah stepped forward and led them onward. After a few moments, they came to an old rope bridge tattered by time. Zachariah started over it with ease. Sir Philip and Lord Donovan stopped.

"Don't be afraid," Zachariah said, glancing over his shoulder. He bounced on the bridge a few times. "It's safe." The two stepped onto the bridge and inched their way across. It sprung and creaked, aching from its years of idleness. The bridge ended on a small landing, which led nowhere but to a rock wall.

Sir Philip squinted. "Is there a path here?" he asked, extending his torch. "It looks like this is it."

"There's a path," Zachariah said. "Follow me." Zachariah led the two through a narrow crevice. They squeezed tightly as the walls and ceiling closed in. Just when it got to where they had to hunch down, Zachariah turned to Donovan.

"My new king, would you like to have the honors?"

"I would," Lord Donovan said.

Zachariah held the torch downward, revealing a tiny slit in the crevice wall. He reached again inside his pouch and brought out a rather ordinary, rusty old key.

"For the first time, Lord Donovan, you shall see the world's greatest treasure."

As Lord Donovan took the key from Zachariah, his hand shook as he fit it into the slot. He turned the key, which resisted, but as he nudged it harder, the key turned all the way, and they all heard a click.

"Now what?" he asked.

"Just wait." Another loud rumble and shaking occurred. It felt as if the walls were about to crash in. But again, they felt the floor move and heard the clanking of pulleys and chains as they descended another shaft. In a moment, they had stopped. The smell of oil permeated the air.

Zachariah moved forward and placed his torch at arm's-length in front of him. "Ready?" he asked. Without waiting for their response, he dropped his torch, and down it went—further and further into a shaft, until flames erupted in a shallow sea of oil.

The three stood there a moment, watching the flames burst before them. "But where is this treasure?" Lord Donovan asked.

"Behind you," Zachariah answered.

King Jared, Aiden, and Xavier exited the newfound chamber and walked back into the temple. Aiden's mind fixed heavily on the things that had just happened, what they had discovered, and what he and his father must do. When all three had entered the temple, King Jared held the pieces of the tapestry in his hand and asked, "What should we do with this? It's ripped. And the books and scrolls, they'll know someone's been here."

"I don't think it matters," Xavier said. "If we are successful tonight, no one will ever enter this room again. Besides, I'm sure Lucifer's subordinates have told him we have been here."

"How," Aiden asked. "I thought we sent them to their doom."

"Not necessarily all of them," Xavier answered. "Remember the one that snuck up behind you and tried to latch itself onto your soul? That's an indication there may be more lurking around somewhere. If word got out, they'll be swarming Whiterock looking for me and my troops in full force."

"Does that mean we could run into more demons on our way out?" Aiden asked.

"It's possible," Xavier replied. "If there are any now within close vicinity, one of my twelve would have informed me by now. But if word has gotten out about us, who knows how many might be sent out to stop us?"

"This complicates things," King Jared said. "Our plans must revolve not only around us but around you and your team as well."

"Don't be concerned about that," Xavier said. "Ask, and the Lord will guide you. I'll converse with Our Lord on our matter, and we will formulate a strategy for ourselves. I'm sure He has a plan. Until then, you'll find your way out of the cave the same way you came in. It's a long haul, especially without commonlears. But remember, my men are out there. Do not be afraid. You will make it in time to see your rescuers."

Aiden cocked his head. "Our rescuers? What do you mean?"

"You'll see," Xavier said. "A search party is returning to look for your remains."

"Remains? Won't they be surprised," King Jared said with a laugh.

Aiden and Xavier smiled. A glorious light enveloped Xavier. He held out his hands as a tray appeared. On the tray were small white cakes. "Manna. Take and eat," he said. "You'll need your strength."

Aiden hadn't thought of food, but suddenly, he was famished. "Thank you," he and King Jared said.

"This should be enough to fill you," he said as the men placed the cakes in a sack attached to their belts. "And here," Xavier said as two small jugs miraculously appeared on the tray. Each jug was just large enough to quench the thirst for one person for one meal.

"You will never find this empty," Xavier said. "Never in your lifetime, nor will your descendants."

The king and his son took the jars, opened the lids, and smelled them.

"What is it?" King Jared asked.

"A Heavenly wine," Xavier noted. "I think you'll enjoy."

"But, I thought you said materializing heavenly things was forbidden?" Aiden asked.

"It's forbidden unless you have permission. Which I do in this case," Xavier answered. The tray disappeared. Then Xavier turned his wrists and nearly clenched his fists. A sword in a belted sheath materialized in each hand. Each sheath and belt was white. One had inscribed upon it, *Aiden, Prince of Whiterock*, and the other, *Jared, King of Whiterock*. Both inscriptions ended with *Servants of the Most High*.

King Jared and Aiden had taken their Heavenly gifts from Xavier. Each unsheathed their new weapon and examined it. Their swords had an intricately woven pearl handle from which a double-edged platinum-colored iron sword—clean, sharp, and shimmering—extended outward. The sword itself had finely crafted decorative artwork emblazoned on it. And on each blade was the inscription: *Servant of the Most High.*

As the king and prince examined their newfound offerings, Xavier held out one more item in each hand. "And you will need these," he said. "These also, you will find, will never run out—in your lifetime or that of your descendants. The light from these torches will burn forever." The king and his son each took a lit torch for their journey to the surface. "The God of Peace will be with you. Jehovah is mighty. Jehovah is victorious. Jehovah is righteous. Our God is strong. He is holy, and He is love." Xavier smiled as he slowly disappeared before their eyes.

Those last words pierced Aiden more deeply than his newly acquired sword ever could. *God is holy, and He is love.*

It had been quite some time since Zachariah had journeyed to the kingdom's treasure chamber, six years, as a matter of fact. But there was something different about it this time.

Zachariah looked around, trying not to let his puzzlement show. Had King Jared actually used this treasure for something within the last six years? Zachariah eyed Philip, who ever-so-briefly glanced at a certain spot on the cave's ceiling.

Zachariah glanced up at what Philip had been coolly observing—a hole in the ceiling. On the ground, directly underneath the hole, seemed to be a smattering of dirt, rock, and scuff marks. As if a stone were thrown into a quiet, still pool of water, Zachariah's memory rippled. Dirt and rock—where a large mound of gold and jewels used to be.

Aiden and King Jared quickly found their way back to the worgraith's lair. "I woke up here," the King said, stopping their walk for a moment. "You were gone, and I was about to search for you. Then, suddenly, Xavier appeared."

King Jared's face lit with awe and wonder. Aiden had never seen his father like this, so vibrant. It was as if he had suddenly transformed from the usual stoic nobleman worn down from years of heavy responsibility into a carefree lad once again. "Aiden, I couldn't believe it. I couldn't believe I was seeing a real angel. Oh, and then there were more. Aiden, it was incredible what just happened, wasn't it? Not since the days of the ancient scrolls has anything like this happened—that I had ever known, anyway. It may never happen again. Cherish this moment, Aiden. It is something worth telling your grandchildren about." The king grabbed the bottle of wine from his pouch. "This will serve as a reminder to our heirs what happened here, long after we are gone." He looked at his torch. "And this."

Aiden didn't know what to say.

King Jared began walking again. "When Xavier led me to the place where I waited for you, he said you were alive, but that you had to awaken on your own. You had to wake in the darkness all alone. He said he couldn't explain any more than that. Isn't that interesting? Do you have any idea why?"

"I know why," Aiden confessed.

"You do?"

Like when he was young, not wanting to confess something that might get him into trouble, Aiden hung his head and grimaced. "Yes."

"Then why?" The king asked.

"I think it was to make me realize something."

"What?"

"What Hell would be like."

"What?" King Jared responded. "Why do you need to know that?"

"Because I'm going there," Aiden said.

King Jared paused. He turned and looked at Aiden with a surprised and worried expression. "What do you mean?" he asked.

"I've hated God since Mother died." A mix of anger and sorrow stirred in Aiden's voice. "I blamed God for that, and I've struggled with even the thought of His existence."

"What?" King Jared asked. He lowered his torch to see Aiden more clearly. The two looked at each other squarely in the eye. His father's eyes displayed disappointment, but his voice only kindness. "Son, I never knew. I—I always thought you believed. I mean, I knew you didn't speak as much about God as I had, but I never knew you struggled with your belief."

Aiden turned and started walking. His father followed. "I've been having recurring dreams about being cast into a fiery pit by those demons. By those very demons we saw today. In my dream, hell is a lot like this cave. When I woke up, I was sure I was dead and lost forever—lost from you, Alicia, and, of course, Mother. I never felt so alone. But I knew I deserved to be separated from you."

Aiden kept walking just ahead of his father. He never looked at him in the eye. Instead, Aiden looked to the ground as he walked.

"When I found out that I was alive, and then the encounter with the demon, and what was going on with Philip and the conspiracy…well…the thought of Heaven and Hell…God and Satan…good and evil…it shook me even more." Aiden stopped. He thought he heard something scatter in the distance. King Jared kept walking and gained a few paces ahead.

"This way, son. Keep talking. I want to hear what you have to say."

Aiden began walking again, letting his father lead. "You're not mad at me?" Aiden asked.

"Of course not," Jared said. "Why would I be mad?"

"Well, because…"

"Because you were doubting the existence of God? Aiden, it's quite common. I think most people have doubted—or struggled—at some point. I know I have."

"*You* have?" Aiden asked.

An echo of footsteps scurried in the darkness. "Heh," a small voice wisped. They paused and heard it again—then another quick scamper. Another short, dainty breath—almost a laugh—escaped the creature as if it were goading the king and his son into a chase. Aiden, struck deeply with fear, sensed a deep evil wash over him.

"I think there are demons among us," Jared whispered.

"What do we do?" Aiden asked.

"Keep moving. I think they're here to scare us more than anything. Remember, Xavier promised us protection, and I have learned the secret of casting them out. Please, tell me more."

A thin red carpet led from the entrance to Whiterock's throne room through the center, flanked on each side by massive marble pillars. The carpet then led up a set of steps to the staging area, where a golden throne upholstered in red velvet graced the center. The molding and pillars were of polished marble, the floor tiled with the same, while the walls and ceiling were unpolished marble. Behind the pillars, large windows lined the wall like guardians and let enormous rays of sunlight fill the room, complementing the sculptures of former kings positioned regally between the pillars.

The large wooden entrance doors latched loudly. The footsteps beyond them clicked and clacked and soon diminished after Zachariah had left Lord Donovan, who remained slouched on the throne. In one hand, the lord held the royal scepter, and in the other, he raised the king's golden chalice and took a sip of eagle's bane wine.

"Father, I have something to tell you," Philip said softly as he paced.

"What is that, son?" the lord asked.

Philip leaned down to whisper, "The hole in the ceiling of the treasure chamber." He looked up as if the hole were right there. "The dirt and rock on the ground." Sir Philip looked down and gestured to the floor in front of Lord Donovan. "If you looked closely, there seemed to be a large pile of treasure missing, and in other places, there seemed to be gaps, as if handfuls of treasure were scooped out. Did you notice?"

"I noticed," the lord replied, waving the hand with the cup. "Perhaps it was just from the king having taken out some of his reserves throughout the years."

"I think it was thievery," Philip snapped. "And I think it was recent. What shall we do about it?"

"We don't know if it was thievery, and we don't know if it was recent." Lord Donovan took another sip of wine. "If it was thievery, we don't know King Jared hasn't already addressed the matter."

"And not have repaired the damage, or had the loot returned to its rightful place?" Philip let that sink in.

Lord Donovan's eyes widened. He sat up straight and set his cup down. "You're right," he breathed. "Why was there a hole in the ceiling? And why wasn't it patched? But no thief could find the treasure; it was too well-hidden. Nor does anyone except for us know it even exists."

Sir Philip clasped his hands together and tapped his two forefingers as he paced.

"And Zachariah is the only one who knows about the treasury," Lord Donovan said.

Sir Philip's lips snaked into a grin. "Could this be why he seems so eager to retire?" He asked. "He must be seized before he exits the castle grounds. I will personally escort some of our knights to his home and see what we can find there."

"So, my hatred and bitterness toward God only festered," Aiden continued. "And within the past few hours, I think it's changing—perhaps. But I don't know."

"What don't you know, Aiden?"

"I don't know what I don't know; that's the problem. Who is God? Why should I trust Him if He's failed me?"

His father did not immediately answer. *Whap! Whap! Whap! Screech!* Aiden flinched at another sudden burst of sound erupting in the darkness. This time, it was louder and closer. Aiden waved his torch toward the commotion. A hundred small shadows shot between the stalactites lining the tunnel. *"Bats!"* Aiden said, hunching. "I *hate* bats!"

His father, however, seemed unfazed. King Jared held his torch out and squinted in the darkness. He watched with a calm curiosity as the tiny creatures maneuvered gracefully around their obstacles. As soon as the bats had flown out of the torchlight and the screeching had faded away, King Jared began walking again. Aiden straightened his posture and followed. King Jared resumed the conversation. "I believe your perspective on God is distorted," the king said. "Based on certain experiences, you've blamed God for things that…"

"Of course He's to blame," Aiden said, his voice still a little shaky. "He's in control." Aiden unintentionally kicked a pebble when his foot scuffed the uneven ground. The sound of the pebble echoed as it bounced off a stalagmite.

"True," King Jared answered softly. "He is in control."

"Then how can you remain so faithful?" Aiden stopped walking. "You've endured Mother's death and the tragic events of the worgraiths—twice! How can you do it? What do you see? How did you overcome your doubt?"

King Jared stopped and turned around to face Aiden. His torch framed his loving countenance, his eyes lit with a gentle spark. "Aiden, it's in times such as these that I rely on God the most. I don't blame Him; instead, I seek Him for comfort, for wisdom, and for strength. I think that's the greatest difference. When I doubted God—when the worgraiths came to Whiterock both this time and the last time—I realized I was left with either cursing God or trusting Him. I decided to trust Him. He proved himself faithful once, and He's doing it again. He's already given us Xavier."

"But who's to blame for the worgraiths in the first place?" Aiden asked angrily. "God is! If God didn't create worgraiths, then we wouldn't be in this mess."

King Jared hung his head. "Maybe," he replied. "Was it God who designed mankind to suffer, or does mankind suffer because of our rebellion and the resulting curse?" The king paused for a moment. "If someone disobeys me, I certainly don't let them get away with it. What's the old saying? 'Let them break your rule, and they'll become your ruler'? I have to be harsh sometimes. But that's the responsibility of being a king."

King Jared paused again. "It isn't always pleasant being king. Many have mistaken me for being cruel and unfair. I can see how The Power Within can believe Satan's deception that God is the evil one," the king said.

"I had never thought of it that way," Aiden said. He looked at the floor of the cavern again. "Putting it in the perspective of a kingdom—I can understand that."

King Jared turned back around and began walking. Aiden followed, briskly catching up to his father.

"But wait a minute. Think about this—we didn't ask to be born in a curse. We have no choice."

"Yes." King Jared nodded. "We didn't ask to be born in a curse—or with a sinful nature—it's like being born with cancer. We don't want it. That's why God made a way where we could not make a way."

"A way for what?" Aiden asked. He suddenly felt a little out of breath.

"A way for redemption." Aiden noticed his father was breathing a little hard from the walk, too. "You know the story. God sent

His Son to pay the price for our sins. That makes Him a good and gracious God."

"What do you mean?"

"The redemption for our sins. We could not do it on our own, and God knew that. It's called grace."

Aiden was quiet for a while. There was so much to take in. "So, how do you explain what happened to mother?"

"Well, death is part of the curse. But because of the atonement, death has no sting—not for those under the blood covenant of God's Son." King Jared continued with a spark in his voice. His step quickened as he stood a little taller. "She's in Heaven. What a joy it must have been for her to enter the gates of paradise." King Jared looked up, as if into Heaven, then to Aiden. Aiden saw a great hope and anticipation on his father's face. King Jared's smile could have lit the entire cavern. He stopped and turned.

Aiden furrowed his brows and stared directly at his father. "So, what about Aeric? I mean, it's just so unfair. He met a brutal death. So did all of those other knights. It's all part of the curse?"

King Jared stepped to Aiden. He could see his father's breath. Again, the king's voice was kind, and his eyes were full of love. "It's all part of the curse. Aiden, you know—having trained so long for your knighthood—what being a knight means. Beyond chivalry and nobility, it is a knight's duty to sacrifice his life for the safety and security of his kingdom. A knight never knows when he must face death. It isn't that much unlike the sacrifice God's Son made for us. He's in a war, too, you know. A war for our souls."

Aiden absorbed the thought. The cave somehow seemed more still and silent than ever before. "A war for our souls?"

King Jared turned around and began to walk. Aiden followed. "A war that his Son's death—and resurrection—has already won. Now, we just have to choose whose side we're on. Do you understand what I am trying to say? How this all fits together? Again, much like a kingdom…like the way The Power Within is rebelling our kingdom right now."

Aiden tried to think this through. "So…God is a good king? I don't know. I mean, if He's so good, then why did He allow this cult to form in the first place? If He's all-knowing, then why did He not just destroy Lucifer so none of this would happen? Why does God allow Satan to exist?"

"Those are hard questions to answer," King Jared admitted.

Aiden noticed the stalagmites were spreading out, and there was enough room for the two to walk abreast, so Aiden sprang up to his father's side. "I think the best way to explain is this. Do you want people to love you?"

"Yes," Aiden replied.

"So does God. That's why He created us. But He doesn't want us to be forced to love Him; He wants us to truly love Him. So, it's our choice. That way, God knows our love is genuine. Apparently, allowing evil to exist is a risk worth the reward of having true love. Rejection is part of the mix. God is experiencing both love and rejection from both humans and angels."

Aiden thought some more. "Okay, so I can choose to follow God. And I have spent these years deciding not to follow God."

"Yes. And so did Lucifer."

Aiden's heart sank. "Wow," he said. "I have something in common with the mind of Lucifer?"

"Yes, wow indeed," King Jared said.

Stalagmites had become even more sparse and were no longer an issue to maneuver around in the dark. With the aid of the torches, Aiden noticed the walls of the cave narrow some ahead as the floor seemed to incline. "It seems Satan and his demons' perception of God somehow skewed, according to what I gathered in that history book and talking with Xavier."

"But that doesn't answer my question, though," Aiden interrupted. "Why do we have to deal with Satan in this world? Why does God allow him to interfere with us?"

"That's another hard question," King Jared confessed again. "I don't know if anyone has the true answer to that. But, to the best of my understanding, part of the curse is letting Satan have a foothold in our world. But I think there's more to it than that. I think maybe it is for our testing so that no rebellion could ever happen—in Heaven—again."

"What do you mean?"

"I think that if Lucifer led a massive amount of angels who saw God face to face—who had access to his very throne—in a rebellion, then it could happen again, and maybe again and again. So, He prevented us from living in Heaven and allowed people this onetime opportunity to pursue Him. Then, if those who loved Him in this world—some who even died for doing so—then they would surely love Him in His kingdom throughout all eternity."

Aiden stopped again. "What if I'm still undecided when I die?"

"Maybe the experiences you've been having are God's way of urging you to make that decision," King Jared said. "He loves you, and He's pursuing your love in return. He wants you to spend eternity with Him in His eternal kingdom, not without Him."

Aiden stopped again. "He's pursuing my love? He's pursuing me?"

"Yes. Because He loves you." Aiden's father seemed a little out of breath again. The grade in front of them steepened even more. A rock lay next to them. "Come sit down, Aiden. Let's rest."

In the quiet of the recovery center, Sir Philip walked silently into Sir Jonathan's room. There, the young warrior lay in a state near death. His skin was pale, and his breathing was heavy, garbled, and sporadic as he rested in a deep coma.

Sir Philip paid no attention to the other warrior in the bed beside Sir Jonathan, just as close to death. The priest of the satanic cult pulled a chair next to his sect brother and whispered slowly and slyly, "It was not supposed to happen like this. I spoke with our lord. His Enemy has interfered with our plans. The worgraiths must attack Whiterock—*tonight*. No foe shall live. You are to come with me, Jonathan. He has chosen you to help me with a significant task. He has asked us to convene with him for further instructions."

Sir Philip sat straight up in his chair, backed away slightly from Sir Jonathan, closed his eyes, and lifted his head and left arm skyward, his right hand placed on Jonathan's forehead.

Then, Sir Philip spoke in an ancient tongue. Surges of energy flowed from Sir Philip's upward-stretched hand, through his body, down through the hand that touched Sir Jonathan, and into his dying body. Sir Jonathan's eyes opened, his color returned, and his breathing returned to normal. Without a word, Jonathan turned his head toward Sir Philip.

"Come, my friend," Sir Philip said. "We have work to do."

Sir Jonathan sat up in bed. He furrowed his eyebrows and pursed his lips. His eyes seemed a bit glazed over as he slowly looked around. His eyes landed on the knight lying in the bed next to him. He was dead.

"Lord Donovan, Sir Brendan is here to see you."

"Ah, send him in."

The sentry opened the doors. A refreshed Sir Brendan entered with vigor in each step and purpose in his eyes. He bowed before his soon-to-be king. "My Lord."

"Your Majesty would do fine."

With a look of surprise on his face, Sir Brendan corrected himself, "Your Majesty."

"You may rise," the lord said. "What is it you request from me?"

"I have come seeking your permission for men to accompany me on another mission to the gorge."

"You wish to hunt more worgraiths?" Lord Donovan asked. "Already? Shouldn't you let your men rest?"

"Your Majesty, I wish to seek and return the bodies of the king and prince."

"Your *former* king and prince."

"Yes…Your Highness. Forgive me—our *former* king and prince."

Lord Donovan slouched a little in his chair as he crossed his legs. "How many men do you need?"

"Considering there may be more worgraiths out there and that we'll try to be as quick as possible, about one hundred should be fine, Sire. Plus, we'll need a funeral carriage and some dragons."

"Ah, yes. Granted. When do you wish to embark?"

"As soon as possible, Your Majesty. I have already asked your son to accompany us. Is that alright?"

"Of course. I wouldn't think of having it otherwise."

"Thank you, Your Highness. Forgive me for not asking your permission to bring him first."

"Forgiveness granted."

Sir Brendan bowed.

"And please hurry," the imminent king said slowly. "Darkness is coming."

Jeff Miller

FIFTEEN

Samuel was almost home. Though the ride should have taken almost no time at all, Samuel decided not to have the young and relatively inexperienced commonlear dash about on their first journey together. It had been cold, but the sun broke through the clouds enough to bring some warmth. When they had gotten home, there was no place to rest his newfound friend except in the same stall where Savannah once laid. Samuel knew that for both of them, it would be too heart-wrenching to have Aeric lie in the same well-worn hay that his mother had left only days ago.

Samuel landed Aeric just outside his home's stables, which, if his home weren't just a stone's throw away, one would assume the elaborate barn to be the house itself. The stables were a two-story thatched-roof building made of strong, dark lumber and large sliding doors.

His house was nothing more than a small, barely two-story charming cottage. The home's roof matched the barn's thatched roof, which peaked steeply and had a chimney on either end of the home. Built from stone, the house incorporated windows bordered with the same sturdy wood as the barn and an arched doorway trimmed in the same wood. Ivy grew up and along the home in places.

Surrounding the two structures were small decorative trees, shrubs, and flowers of all kinds. Leading from the barn to the house was a stone walkway. The stones had come from the nearby brook, where the current had smoothed them flat.

For Samuel, his home would be as close to heaven as anyone could imagine. Zachariah had plenty of his own land, but not nearly as much as a lord or baron. He had a simple farm where he raised enough food for Samuel, himself, and their commonlears along with enough rolling pasture for their animals, for scenery, and for quiet's sake. The view of Whiterock Castle was mesmerizing, like a fine painting.

No one would assume one of the most powerful men in all of Whiterock lived there, and that was just the way Zachariah wanted it, no attention drawn to him, though everything about it was pristine and well-made. His humility and his meticulousness were among the king's many reasons for choosing Zachariah as his personal advisor.

As Samuel landed, he was happy to hear the bleating of sheep, a few soft moos from the cattle, and the clucking and scurrying of chickens practically under his feet. The brook nearby gently rippled in a soothing and familiar rhythm.

Samuel, still a little sore, gently dismounted Aeric. "Hold on, Aeric. I'll get you some new hay and…" Aeric groaned sadly and nudged Samuel. "What's the matter?" Aeric shook his head, and Samuel slumped his shoulders. "I understand," Samuel said. "Come inside; you can sleep in my room tonight."

Samuel expected to see his grandfather walk out of the house at any moment. He had spent much of the ride picturing just how his grandfather might come out of the house, amazed that his grandson was home so soon.

As Samuel wondered where his grandfather was, he placed both of his crutches under his shoulders. As soon as he did, he noticed that except for some remaining soreness from the bruises, he could walk—still slowly and gingerly—without them. *What is going on? I was nearly dead. Now, it's almost as if nothing ever happened.* Samuel slowly started walking toward his home with Aeric by his side.

When King Jared and Aiden had their fill of manna and wine, the king rose from the cavern floor. "Ready? We still have a long way to go."

"Yes," Aiden said. "Let's get out of this cave." Aiden heard a scurry behind him. He turned with a jolt and with a wave of his torch, watched a hunched figure run from behind a set of large stalactites and into the shadows.

"Show yourself," King Jared commanded in a booming voice. "Are you friend or foe—angel or demon?"

A low growl was the only reply.

"You shall not frighten us, demon," the king said. "For my Lord and King is still Lord and Master over you!"

The shadow roared, and behind it emerged a soft light which revealed the silhouette of the monster. Within the light, a human figure appeared that was instantly recognizable as one of Xavier's guardians, but not one they had met before. He held his sword downward above the demon, and the demon faced the guardian, cowering. "Where is your sword, devil?" Ariel asked.

The demon lost its balance as it unsheathed its sword, aiming it upward toward Ariel.

"Who are you, and why are you here?" Ariel asked.

The evil spirit clenched its teeth, growled, and replied in a high-pitched wheeze, "I have no name."

"You once had a name," Ariel reminded it. "We were all given names."

"I have a name no more," the ghoulish fiend cried.

Dismissing this remark, Ariel asked, "How many more of you are there?"

"Just me. I am alone," the ragged spirit hissed.

"Liar!" Ariel shouted. "How many more of you are there?"

"None. One. Thousands. Who knows?" it answered with a high-pitched cackle.

Ariel studied the monster. "You don't know?" he asked. Ariel swiftly brought his sword down on the demon's. He moved so fast that the monster's sword flew from its hand before it knew what to do. Then, prodding his sword against the demon's throat, Ariel asked, "You *really* don't know?"

"I…I…," the demon stuttered.

"And don't even think about trying to use that dagger in your belt," Ariel warned.

"I…I…don't know for sure. My master only knows."

"Any idea *about* how many of you are around here?" Ariel asked again.

The unnamed rebel smiled as if it had been keeping a dirty little secret. "Thousands, tens of thousands," it said with a victorious chortle.

Ariel jabbed his sword harder. If it were a human, the spirit's skin would have punctured.

"Ahhhhh. I think you are in for quite the fight tonight," it said, the sword straining its ability to talk.

"I don't doubt it," Ariel said. "Now, answer me one more question. Should I penetrate your throat, or should I let you go?"

"It does not matter," the evil angel answered. "We will win. My master will be ruler over Whiterock, and then, with a little patience, over time, we will take this world over completely."

The twisted, mocking laugh that followed didn't sit well with Jehovah's warrior angel. He speared the enemy's throat, and Satan's angel quickly vanished into oblivion.

Aiden and King Jared were speechless. Ariel placed his sword upright in front of him, his piercing gaze transfixed on Aiden and King Jared as the guardian angel faded from their sight.

As darkness suddenly enveloped the cave once again, the king and his son stood still in the now cold and motionless cavern, the flickering flame from their supernatural torches the only movement. King Jared said after a moment, "I think we'd better hasten our journey. We must not underestimate the gravity of this situation. We need to find the knights and form a plan as soon as possible."

Samuel found his home in shambles. Furniture was displaced, doors were wide open, and tracks of mud were everywhere.

"Who *did* this? Grandfather, are you here? Are you alright?"

Samuel searched the house for Zachariah. "Oh, no, I wonder if they found…" Samuel darted to the kitchen and noticed the rug underneath the table had not moved. *But just in case*, he thought. Samuel upended the kitchen table and pushed the rug aside. He slid his finger into a knothole in one of the floorboards and pulled, opening a secret compartment.

The front door suddenly flew open and slammed into the wall. "Samuel!" a voice boomed, "You're wanted for thievery. Come out now; we know you're here."

"What?"

"You've stolen the king's gold, and we caught you in the process of hiding it," one of Lord Donovan's knights bellowed as he made his way into the kitchen.

"No, wait, you're wrong, I was…"

A slithery voice behind the knight interrupted, "You were what, Samuel? I was in the recovery center paying my last respects to my dying friends when my father summoned me to arrest you. I will make this worth the effort of your having disturbed my one and only chance to say goodbye to my friends while they were still alive; that's for sure," Sir Philip said.

"I knew there was a reason I hated you," Philip continued. "After our very king and his son—your best friend—died today, you had the audacity to do this. Tell me, *squire*, did you and your grandfather decide to seize this opportunity after recent events, or had you planned this for a long time?"

"You evil…" Samuel said furiously, too angry for words. He leaped toward Philip, but Samuel's still-sore legs got the best of him. A quick jolt of pain shot through his legs and brought him to his knees before he could lay the wretch to the ground. Philip's men drew their swords, pointing them at Samuel.

"Take him back to the dungeon with his grandfather," Philip ordered.

"Wait!" Samuel protested. "See for yourself. The king's treasure is not here. We were the ones who were robbed…"

"Silence!" Philip ordered. He looked over at a large, gruff knight. "Search the underground cache for evidence."

Philip crouched down at Samuel's level. "I hope for Alicia's sake there is nothing to find here, *squire.*" Philip's evil eyes bore into Samuel. "It would grieve my bride awfully to learn that you betrayed her—and the memory of her father and brother."

"Here it is, Sire. Is this what you're looking for?" the constable inquired, pulling up a slightly weighty chest just small enough to carry with one arm. He set the cache on the ground next to Samuel. "There's more like it down there."

"You snake! You set me up!"

"How? How could I have gained access to the king's gold? I only learned of its existence this afternoon. Your grandfather showed me and my father where it was. It was then that I saw something suspicious. And he's the only one other than the king who knows where the treasury is hidden. So, naturally, my father summoned me and my troops here. Is this the king's gold or not, *squire?*" Philip demanded. "Answer me now, and it better be the truth, or you and your grandfather will receive a worse punishment for lying!"

"No!"

"It is yours then?" the constable asked.

"It must be. There's no way I or my grandfather could have..."

"It must be? It is, or it is not!" Philip disrupted. "Is this yours? Have you seen this before?"

Samuel remained quiet.

"Is this yours?" Philip asked again.

"I do not know," Samuel replied. "I have never seen it."

"Then it is not yours?" the constable asked.

"It must be. It was in our cache," Samuel answered. "My grandfather is an honest man!"

"Is it the king's?" Philip questioned. "Let's see."

He took a few steps toward the chest and opened the lid with the tip of his sword. Inside the container were ancient coins and jewels as pristine as if they were just fashioned that day. But a mark was clearly visible on the inside of the lid. It was the royal family's seal.

"No, this can't be!" Samuel said. "You set me up! You thief!"

"Take him away," Philip ordered. Then he turned to the knight who found the box. "Bring up the rest of the cache. We will need it as evidence. I will personally see that my father has these in his possession."

"No!"

Without care, the men roughly heaved Samuel up by the arms and dragged him outdoors. Pain surged through Samuel's body, confirming that he truly had not yet recovered. When Philip's knights noticed Samuel gritting his teeth and wincing, they roughed him up even more. Sir Philip looked out the back door and noticed the diminutive commonlear, who had watched the whole episode.

Hmph. Philip walked out the door, took his sword, and held it to the commonlear's throat. Aeric flinched. "So, you're Savannah's son? You'd better find a new master," he said. "I don't think you will ever see this one again." Philip sheathed his sword and walked away.

The faint roar of rolling water grew louder as a dim light penetrated the cave. "Ah, almost there," King Jared said. "Let us rest again, just for a moment, before our last leg."

King Jared and Aiden sat on the hard, wet ground, having hardly spoken since their last break. Aiden had tried to suppress a question, to bury it deep, but he couldn't. "I've felt trapped in bitterness and rage over Mother's death, and now over Aeric. But I can't seem to let go of blaming God for making these things happen. So how do I trust God to set me free when He's the source of my bitterness and rage? No matter how much I want these emotions to stop, I can't make them stop. I hate it!"

The king thought for a moment. "Perhaps the best place to start is to forgive God," King Jared said.

"What? What for? Why should I forgive God? Is He sorry for what He's done?"

"No, He has nothing to be sorry for, remember?" The king answered with a slight smile. "It's about letting go of your anger. It's about letting go of trying to figure God out. We can't figure out everything. He is such a mystery."

Aiden looked away from his father. "I know that's not what you want to hear," King Jared said. "I understand. But that's the first place to start a right relationship with Him. Not knowing, but discovering, bit by bit, as time goes on. Maybe God won't answer all your questions, but He'll reveal Himself to you in other ways as He sees fit. In wonderful ways. Do you understand?"

Aiden groaned.

"I don't think He really wanted to place us under a curse, Aiden, but He is King. He can't just let mankind rebel and get away with it."

Aiden slumped his shoulders as King Jared tried to catch Aiden's eyes. "Because of the curse, we have to face harshness and brutality, sickness and disease, and such unfairness like the timing of Aeric's death and your mother's death. We have to face The Power Within and these worgraiths."

King Jared paused for a moment, searching for words. "Think of it this way," he continued, "death leads to life."

Aiden scrunched his face. "What?"

His father sighed as his face brightened a little. "Although sin and death are a curse on our lives, we are not cursed to live this way forever—that is, so long as we become God's children. Death is actually freedom for us."

Aiden sighed again. "But why did she have to die when she did? If God were really good, He would have prevented it; He would have known it wasn't her time. She was so young. *I* was so young!" Aiden's eyes filled with tears.

"I know, Aiden. You're right. It doesn't seem fair for it to have happened when it did, and I still grieve, too. I don't have an answer. But we can't live our lives dwelling on this one event, living in misery. God wants *our* lives to go on, and He wants to be part of them."

Aiden wiped his tears.

"He wants to bless you; He wants to fill your life with that freedom you've been searching for and give you joy. But your anger and unforgiveness has been keeping that from happening—it has been blocking your life from moving forward. The first step to freedom is forgiving God, letting go of your anger towards Him. Then, ask Him to forgive you."

"Forgive me?" Aiden said in a broken voice. "For what?"

King Jared did not answer.

Aiden let out another sigh and slumped. He looked at the ground. "There's so much, isn't there?" he asked. "There's so much that I've done. The bitterness and hatred…my attitude…my pride…making her death all about me." Aiden thought some more. "And just the mere fact that my heart's not right with God."

King Jared pleaded, "Make it right, Aiden. And you will have new life—now, and forever."

Aiden was quiet for a moment and then said, "Come on, let's get out of here."

"Sir Philip, where have you been? I've been looking for you. We've been assembling to retrieve the bodies of the king and prince. Are you ready?"

"Almost, Sir Brendan. I have had some important business to attend to. I should be ready soon."

"Good, meet us at the usual place between the castle and stables."

"Yes," Philip said. "It would be an honor. Oh, and will it take long?"

It was hardly worth the effort to throw Samuel into the dungeon. The very same sentry who slammed the cell doors and locked him in came back in a few moments to let him out. "Come on; our new king doesn't want to waste any time," the guard said.

"New king? I thought…"

"Silence!" the guard demanded. "He'll be your king soon—well, depending on whether he'll let you live long enough." He and another sentinel took Samuel by the arms, gripping tightly. This time he tried not to give them the satisfaction of wincing. They escorted him up the stairs and through many corridors that Samuel had never known existed. He was eventually led down a familiar hallway.

The massive, foreboding chamber doors creaked as they opened. Samuel couldn't help but wince as he beheld Lord Donovan sitting on King Jared's throne, wrapped in royal garb and wearing the king's crown as if it were his own. Anger filled Samuel as he clenched his teeth and looked down.

If that wasn't enough to seize Samuel with hatred, anger filled him even more as his once proud and noble grandfather was now hunched over like an abused dog. It appeared someone had dragged him through the mud. His grandfather's ripped robes were stained with blood.

Zachariah turned his filthy head and gazed at Samuel. Samuel saw a scared and bewildered man behind the matted mane and bloodied brow.

Samuel felt his chest tighten with rage. "How can you do this?" he screamed at the lord. "You traitor!"

"Silence! *You* are the traitor, young squire!" Lord Donovan said. "And I suggest you not speak to your king in such a manner. It seems you have a penchant for being brash, or so I'm told. You gave my men—and my son—a difficult time. Philip said you tried to attack him. Is this true?"

Samuel didn't know how to reply. He glanced over at his grandfather, who looked back, dumbfounded.

"I came home and—"

"Silence!" the lord ordered. "I asked you a question. I do not want to hear anything other than the answer. Did you try to attack my son or not?"

Samuel gave up. There was no other way to answer the weighted question. He hung his head and quietly answered, "Yes."

"And were you caught hiding the king's stolen treasure?"

"No!"

"Liar!" Lord Donovan responded furiously. "I have sworn testimony from witnesses," he said as he gestured his hand at the knights around the room. "And you, old man, what do you have to say for yourself?"

"I have endured repeated beatings, my lord. And I have not changed my plea. I am innocent. If I wanted the king's gold, I would have accepted the throne."

Scowling, Lord Donovan squirmed as he straightened. "You'd do anything to hide your guilt," the lord eventually replied. "You'd rather endure a beating than the shame of admitting stealing from the king."

"My Lord," Zachariah said, "you know I am a good and honest man. The king is my friend."

"The king is dead!" Lord Donovan screamed as he rose from his seat and pointed the heavy scepter. "And for whatever reason, you did not want the throne, but you couldn't resist taking some of the king's reserves for yourself. You thought no one would catch on to your plan, but evidence of your deeds was easy to see."

"You mean the hole in the ceiling and dirt and rocks where a pile of the king's treasure used to be? I saw it, too!"

"Of course you did," the lord replied. "You caused it! My son and I saw it, too. Thankfully for us, you were careless enough to forget to cover your tracks. And we found the stolen reserves in your possession. So, clearly you and your grandson are the thieves!"

Lord Donovan sat back down. "Therefore," the steward pounded the scepter on the floor, "I banish you from the kingdom. You will spend the rest of your miserable lives in the hot springs of the San Kor Talon Islands. If I receive word that you have somehow found your way back inside continental Whiterock, I'll have you thrown into the dungeon for the rest of your lives!"

Samuel's mind swirled. "No!" he screamed, "We are innocent! You can't do this!"

"Silence, or I will change my mind and have you thrown into the dungeon now!" Lord Donovan demanded. "Be thankful that I am showing you mercy and haven't sentenced you to death! Take them away!"

The guards grabbed Samuel and Zachariah and lifted them off the ground. Samuel wriggled his way free and kicked one of the guards, but the brute whacked Samuel over the head with the pommel of his sword. He fell to the ground.

"No!" Zachariah screamed. Within seconds, Zachariah's guard had the tip of his blade a hairsbreadth from Zachariah's face. Samuel groaned. The guards lifted and shoved him and his grandfather out of the king's throne room.

"I don't like this," a knight said to Sir Brendan. "There are worgraiths still out there, and the sky is getting dark, and it'll be even darker once those menacing clouds move in. And it feels like it may snow."

Sir Brendan checked the halter on his commonlear. "I know," he said. "But we have to do this, and we have to do it now. There's no time to waste. I have this feeling, this feeling of urgency. I can't explain it, but it's…" Sir Brendan looked back at the knight. He could clearly see that his subordinate didn't understand; it was no use trying to explain. "Just make sure your men are ready with the hearse," he said.

"Yes sir," the assistant replied.

Sir Brendan finished checking his commonlear. "I don't know," he said to his dragon, Caleb. "It just seems like God is telling me something. I don't know what exactly, but…"

Caleb moaned worriedly.

"Yeah, I'm scared, too," Sir Brendan said.

Exhausted, King Jared and Aiden finally reached the mouth of the cave. Aiden knew his experiences in the depths would change him forever, and once he passed through the waterfall into the familiar realm of the surface, Aiden would have to face his biggest challenge—reclaiming his father's throne from insurgents bent on a satanic creed.

But how?

A dim blue light barely penetrated through the waterfall. Aiden could feel the mist from the icy waters gripping his skin. "Isn't there another way through?" he asked.

"No, son, I don't think so."

Just then, a beautiful male voice spoke. "Go ahead."

King Jared and Aiden looked at each other in wonder and then peered behind them. There was no one. They looked in front of them and noticed the waters open like a curtain.

"Go through," the voice gently said.

Too amazed to speak, Aiden and his father went through the invisible curtain. Coming out the other end warm and dry, they continued along the same path on which they entered. Making it to a spot above the falls, King Jared said, "I think we should take a moment to praise our God for another miraculous experience, Aiden. God is surely with us. See, God *is* good."

Aiden managed to smile, but the rest of his face remained frozen. He nodded awkwardly.

Alicia had thought taking her commonlear out for a ride would make her feel better, just like it always had. But the refreshing open air didn't clear away the horrific images replaying endlessly in her mind: the bloody sight of dead and wounded soldiers returning from a horrific battle, her father and brother both meeting a gruesome and untimely death, and Philip erupting in an unreasonable fit of jealous rage.

She had returned from her short ride, withdrawing to the sanctuary of her room. She had tried praying, singing, weaving, even napping. But it was no use. She paced back and forth. And Brianna, in whom she could always confide, was still busy helping at the recovery center.

Alicia's other attendants had knocked on her door, asking if she was alright and offering her some food and company, but she politely refused. Perhaps later. She scribbled her scattered and angry thoughts in a diary, which helped some.

She stood on her balcony, gazing at the pending sunset. Her breath was a thick haze that danced through the cold air. As she wrapped Philip's soft, warm, heavy cape around her, she hoped it would help remind her she would not be living so alone—so long as *he* returned alive. She also hoped that as it hugged around her, it might convince her that his outburst was only from the stresses of war, not true unbridled jealousy.

Still shivering, she replayed Philip's rush of anger over and over in her mind; she couldn't shake it, no matter how hard she tried.

Alicia startled as a sudden blast of noise and energy came from behind and roared past her tower. Knights on their steeds flew overhead, accompanying a meticulously carved ebony carriage three-times the length of a regular coach. She knew full well why a hearse was leaving, surrounded by a group of knights. Alicia's heart sank. Her mind spun. She closed her eyes tight.

"Dear God," she sighed, "I pray for the safe return of those knights. May there be no more bloodshed. Help them all return safely. Especially Philip."

Philip. There it was again—the stirring in her spirit, a tension that hinted his surge of anger was just a foretaste of what was yet to come. An idea not her own flooded her mind: she must take her time and not hurry the wedding. *There may be more to discover about Philip. Could Aiden and Samuel have been right all along?*

She reached for the pendant Philip gave her, took it off, and looked at it. *Throw it,* an inner voice told her. *Throw it from the balcony.*

What would I tell Philip when he asked why I wasn't wearing it? How would he react?

She looked more closely at the locket. She felt evil emanating from it like invisible smoke. *What is this? It feels like—like it's— charmed or something.*

Alicia looked up. In no time, the line of men on commonlears and the funeral carriage had dissolved into the sunset like powder in the breeze. The bottom of the clouds rolling in reflected a beautiful mix of white, gold, orange, and red as the colors on the billowy mass faded upward into a menacing charcoal gray.

Still holding onto the necklace, Alicia studied it. Barely able to withstand its sudden surge of energy, she let go, turned around and walked into her room. Its power subsided. Perhaps it was her mind playing tricks on her.

Her thoughts were interrupted by the sound of another set of dragons hauling something large. She turned around. They were escorting a different type of carriage, one usually used to transport prisoners. *Prisoners? Now? At this time of day? Who could it be?*

A bitter wind lashed through the nearly naked forest. Thick, ominous charcoal clouds continued to blanket the sky.

"So, it's never supposed to go out, ever?" Aiden asked.

"That's what Xavier said. And neither is the wine."

"So, what do we do with them once we get home?"

"As far as the wine, I don't know. But the torches—I think I know just the place."

Aiden gave his father a puzzled look.

"Someplace you have not seen yet," King Jared said. "The treasury."

"Oh, you were going to tell me about that."

"I suppose now is as good a time as any." King Jared replied. "The treasury is in a man-made cave under the castle. It's quite an ordeal to find it."

"So, doesn't it already have torches?" Aiden asked.

"Actually, no. Not quite. There's a natural oil well down there, Aiden."

"Really?"

"Yes. We created a mechanism that opens the well just enough to let out a bit of oil into a trench around the treasure. The trench is shallow enough that it will burn up all the oil in enough time to get what we need or put in more. But let's say we need to be in the treasury longer than the allotted time, which has happened only once or twice. Then we have to exit the chamber and enter back in again."

"What do you mean? I don't understand," Aiden asked.

"A gate that pours oil out around the treasury opens the well. It's connected by a set of pulleys triggered when someone lowers into the chamber. Kind of like our drawbridge over the moat. Clever, eh? My great-grandfather thought of that. He was a brilliant man."

Aiden's attention fixed on the pleasant warmth of the torch he carried. "Tell me more about your great-grandfather. And you. I want to know more."

King Jared turned, delighted. "I've never told you much about myself, have I, Aiden?"

"No," he replied. "Nor have you ever talked much about our family—at least not in any personal way."

"Oh," King Jared said. He handed Aiden some more manna and took a bite himself. "Then, why don't I tell you? Where should I start?"

Since their banishment required them to leave continental Whiterock, Samuel and Zachariah had expected an incredibly long journey. But they began their descent not long after having taken flight.

Zachariah and his grandson looked at each other, still bound at their hands and feet and gagged. Across from where they sat, a guard kept watch over them.

"You will find out where we are going in just a moment," the guard said. The coach landed swiftly on the ground. Samuel and Zachariah hardly felt a bump. The prisoners heard nothing more than the familiar sound of dragon feet and wheels on a smoothly paved stone road.

The carraige jolted as soon as they crossed what seemed to be a wooden bridge and then returned to a stone pathway. The driver commanded the dragons to slow down. When the coach came to a complete stop. Zachariah heard muffled voices but could not tell who they were.

There was some shuffling in the driver's seat. The guard moved forward and removed the gags from their mouths.

"Are you going to just kill us now and get it over with?" Zachariah scowled.

The guard glanced quickly at the old man with a sudden, warm grin and said nothing.

"It would be easier for the supposed, yet-to-be crowned king to just kill the two of us rather than expend resources sending us away," Zachariah said. "If this is the case, then, of course, out here there could be no witness, no record of our murder."

The guard smirked and shook his head. "No," he said in a friendly tone. "You'll see in just a moment." He cocked his head slightly, as if trying to figure out what was going on outside.

Zachariah squinted at the guard, trying hard to figure this out. Then he heard the clattering of boots echoing toward the carriage. Samuel wriggled in his seat, still bound.

"Hold it," the sentry said in an unusually kind tone. "Calm down and stay seated."

"Stay seated and die!" Samuel said. "If I'm going to die, I'd rather die fighting!" Samuel sprang up.

"Sit down!" The sentry shoved Samuel back in his place.

Samuel abruptly fell back in his seat, and before he could make another try at getting up, the door opened. Light from torches revealed the driver, who greeted them with a warm smile.

A voice from behind the driver spoke in a soft, warm tone. "You needn't be afraid, Samuel. It seems we have much to talk about."

Zachariah could only see the silhouette of a man wearing what was easily distinguishable as the robes of nobility. Immediately behind him was a grand manor with lamps leading to its door, a warm and inviting manor Zachariah and Samuel both knew very well.

The guard then freed the two prisoners from their bondage. A calmness washed over Zachariah. The driver held out his hand and helped Zachariah out of the coach as Samuel silently followed. As they did, the shadowy figure stepped closer; his face became clear in the torchlight.

"Thank God the knights who watch over my barony, ones whom I know and trust dearly, happened to be the ones ordered to send you and Samuel on your merry way to the hinterlands. Please, you are my guests for as long as you need to stay. No one will ever know you are here."

Zachariah's heart melted. He placed his hands on the shoulders of the man standing in front of him. "Sir Franklin, my friend. I am so glad to see you."

Sir Brendan led the knights over the gorge in the same formation as King Jared had, hoping that this would give the men ample time to retreat or prepare for battle if a worgraith shot up from a hiding place below.

The dim of twilight mixed with the overcast sky made scouting worgraiths nearly impossible. But Sir Brendan and his men were intent on their mission. Something deep inside was still telling him that returning the bodies of the king and his son had to be done now.

In a distant ledge of the gorge, father and son noticed little fiery lights flying in the distance. "That looks like a funeral procession," King Jared said.

"Or a scouting party."

"Xavier was right!" King Jared's eyes lit up. "Remember, he said there would be a search party for us. And there they are. Sir Brandon is with them; I recognize Caleb!"

A great shadow moved slowly in the depths of the gorge. "Father, look!" Aiden said.

King Jared and Aiden watched in horror as the king waved his torch furiously. King Jared tried to yell a warning but found he had no voice. "Could the angel of God not have foreseen this?" King Jared whispered. "Could God himself...?"

The menacing worgraith moved slowly and stealthily like a shark. The king and his son stood frozen as they watched tiny lights scamper in the dark like the sparks in their fire. Then, they saw one massive flame rise out of the darkness and set the hearse and condolears ablaze. They shot down through the chasm, engulfed in flames. Torches fell throughout the gorge like sparks from a blacksmith's shop.

"Father, look at how many men have just fallen to their deaths!"

"No, wait, son!" King Jared said with a hope in his voice. "The knights are dropping their torches. They're freeing their hands for battle. God be with them."

King Jared and Aiden watched as several still-glowing embers encircled the giant. However, one torch in particular seemed to encircle the dragon and wave its torch as if signaling to a group of men. It wasn't Sir Brendan.

"What is that soldier doing?"

"I don't know, Aiden. It's hard to tell from here," the King said. "Dear God, let them win."

The signal seemed to direct several men to back off.

But why? Aiden thought. Though it was hard to see clearly in the darkness, Aiden could tell by the brief illumination of torches, the war shouts from the men and screams from the worgraith, that those who remained fought hard and fast. The worgraith's blaze illuminated the battle even more for a moment as it lit many on fire. More soldiers and dragons fell through the canyon like flaming arrows. But in a matter of moments, the screams of men and commonlears had ended. Aiden jumped as the worgraith breathed flames to illuminate the canyon as it scoured the floor for its fallen meal. It gathered what it could and disappeared into the darkness.

"The search party that Xavier promised us failed," the king said, choking back tears. "How can this be?"

"See?" Aiden yelled as he clenched his fists and kicked dirt into the fire. "God *is* useless!"

EIGHTEEN

After Samuel and Zachariah changed into fresh, clean clothes, they accompanied Sir Franklin to his dining hall for a meal.

Quietness fell after Zachariah told Sir Franklin everything that had happened since Aeric, Sir Franklin's only son, had died at the hands of a hideous worgraith.

"Sire," Samuel said, breaking the silence. "If it means anything to you, I named my new dragon Aeric."

Sir Franklin's face brightened a little. "You did?"

"Yes. He happens to be Savannah's son."

Sir Franklin smiled. "You don't know how that makes me feel." His smile widened. "So, where is your new dragon?"

"I don't know," Samuel answered. "If I'm banished forever, then I assume he returned to his stall at the royal stables."

"We have to get Aeric back to you," Sir Franklin said.

"But how?"

"Maybe there's a way one of my men can sneak him out tonight. That should be fairly easy. They could say he escaped or something."

"No," Zachariah said. "It could seem suspicious."

"Maybe not," Samuel said. "Maybe they would believe he felt a connection with me. They could say he must have escaped to find me or something."

Sir Franklin took a sip of tea. "Your grandfather is right," he said. "It might seem suspicious. Your dragon is too young and inexperienced."

"Then I will get him myself," Samuel replied.

"No, you will not," his grandfather said.

"Why?" Samuel asked.

"Why do you think?" Zachariah shot back. "We're safe here. We have food, lodging, and new clothes. No one knows we're here, and it's going to stay that way. We're not going back to the castle— especially you! That would be utterly foolish."

Samuel sat back in his chair, doing his best to withhold his anger and frustration.

Sir Franklin calmly sat back in his chair. He scratched his chin. "How about we *all* go back to the castle? And we take some others with us?"

"What? Others? Who?" Zachariah asked as he leaned forward. "The handful of knights that brought us here? And the few of us do what?"

"Oh, not just them; all the noblemen and knights in the kingdom," Sir Franklin answered. "All we can muster."

"*And?*" Zachariah asked, waiting for a reply.

"And… revolt," Sir Franklin said, as if he were suggesting something as simple as flying through the countryside.

Zachariah and Samuel looked at each other. "A revolt?" Samuel asked.

"Yes," Sir Franklin said. "I know all the other noblemen would die for the honor and memory of our beloved king and prince—and to keep Whiterock out of the hands of Sir Donovan. No one trusts him."

Zachariah looked down. "King Jared had. And so did I."

Sir Franklin looked at Zachariah and said, "I hope you know that we all had wished you had accepted our king's offer. You certainly have our confidence—and you had His Majesty's."

Zachariah shook his head then looked up. "I know I heard God tell me He had something important for me to do, a place for me, but I thought He meant it was for something else, something…" Then his eyes widened. With renewed vigor, he said, "When do we revolt?"

A gleam sparkled in Sir Franklin's eyes. "Tonight."

"Tonight?" Zachariah asked. "Do you think we can pull this off tonight?"

Sir Franklin tilted his eyes to the ceiling then leaned forward and looked at Zachariah. "I think if you, my men, and I split up, we can send the word out to all the nobles tonight. But the uprising couldn't occur until dawn at the earliest. It will be a sleepless night."

"It would be a sleepless night regardless," Zachariah said.

"What about me?" Samuel asked. "What can I do?"

A hush fell over the table.

His eyes darted between his two elders. "Just three of us squires fought two worgraiths. That has to mean *something* about my fighting skills."

There was still nothing but silence from his grandfather. "I'm part of this," Samuel continued with fervor. "Aiden's dead." He looked at Sir Franklin. "And Aeric's dead—my two blood brothers." Then he looked again at his grandfather. "I'm the only one left. Let me *do* something!"

With determination ablaze in Zachariah's eyes and a sharp grin crossing his face, he leaned toward his grandson, pointed his finger at him, and said, "Go back to the castle—carefully, quietly. You're our spy. Tell the other knights encamped there—the ones you can trust—what's going on and tell them to be ready to meet us in the air. Then, find Alicia, protect her, and make sure she's kept safe. She can't be anywhere near Philip, and she certainly can't get caught in the crossfire. Bring her back here safely—with Aeric. Kidnap her if you must."

Alicia sat up, screaming in terror. Her heart raced as her eyes and mouth opened wide in panic. She gasped deeply, trying to catch her breath. She was alone in her room, and the reality of being separated from her family for the rest of her life suddenly brought her to tears again.

Someone pounded furiously on her door. Alicia jumped, and her heart raced. "My lady, my lady, are you alright? We heard you screaming. Alicia…?"

"Yes, Brianna. I'm alright," she said, catching her voice. "It was a nightmare."

"Oh, dear," Brianna said. "Do you need something?"

"No, I'll be alright," Alicia said, whisking away her tears.

"Are you sure, my lady?"

"Yes, thank you." Alicia's voice still shook.

"Alright, your highness; please let us know if you need anything."

"Thank you," Alicia said. "I will."

As Alicia heard Brianna's footsteps echo down the hall, she suddenly felt a strange, dark sensation—a presence almost—seem to surround her. Perhaps it was just the lingering sensation from the nightmare or her dimly lit room and the chill of the night. Maybe it was the horrors of the day.

Or maybe … Alicia touched the charm around her neck. Was it really cursed?

Alicia thought for a moment and decided it was finally time. The only way to get rid of her fear and loneliness and to think clearly was to find some company. Maybe Brianna hadn't gone too far.

She threw a robe over her nightgown and headed for her door. Something caught Alicia's attention from the corner of her eye. There was something moving out her window—a flicker of torches in the sky.

She ran to her terrace. There was no hearse. It couldn't be them; but then again, if they met a worgraith…Philip! Alicia raced out her bedroom door and down the stairs as quickly as she could. She needed to see if Philip made it back alive.

Sir Franklin had arranged for commonlears to be readied for Samuel and Zachariah, and in no time, he had also found armor and chain mail to fit them both.

Sir Franklin was the first to arrive outside the stables. There, three armored commonlears awaited them.

"Which one is mine?" Samuel asked.

"The one on the end, there," Sir Franklin said as he pointed to the dark blue commonlear. Samuel started toward the indicated commonlear, but Sir Franklin put up a hand. "Samuel, your grandfather and I highly respect you. You know that, don't you?"

"Yes, Sire," Samuel replied. Until now, though, he hadn't.

Sir Franklin placed both hands on Samuel's shoulders. "I believe with all my heart that God has placed His hand upon you. For whatever reason, Samuel, He has given you special favor above our former prince and my own beloved son."

Sir Franklin looked away. Samuel felt Sir Franklin loosen his grip. The nobleman's eyes, red and watered, came back to meet his. "I must confess it pains me not to see you three young blood brothers riding together. I do not understand it, and…" His voice quaked. "I still wrestle with accepting my son's death…to never see him fulfill what I thought to be his destiny. I've always thought that the three of you would do great things. But apparently God meant…"

Sir Franklin stopped. Gaining his voice, he gripped Samuel's shoulders again, giving them a quick yet gentle shake. "I've always seen something special in you…and I saw it in Aeric and Aiden." He let go of Samuel, who felt a lump form in his throat.

"But I believe you are alive for a reason, Samuel. God still has great plans for you. I can feel it bursting in my heart." Sir Franklin pointed at Samuel with a fire in his eyes. "You are to be a tremendous leader in this kingdom. God has, is, and will continue to surround you with His angels." Sir Franklin paused again. He blinked back a few tears. His voice was still soft, but not as trembling. "Wait for us after you have brought Alicia here, Samuel. We want you to join us in battle."

Samuel didn't know what to say. He felt remorse for his friends, yet it was refreshing to know that although barely a man, he had earned the admiration of one of the kingdom's most highly respected men. But did God have a special hand on him?

Samuel heard the footsteps of his grandfather approaching from behind, but he did not let it interrupt what he was about to say. "Sir Franklin, surely, if anyone, God's hand—if it would have been on anyone—it would have been on Aeric. He was the one true believer among the three of us. After all that I had said and thought about God…I barely believed. And I know Aiden struggled."

"Samuel," his grandfather said softly as he walked next to Sir Franklin, "I know, and I have always known, that God has put His hand on you. I have waited for this moment ever since you were born. Do not fear; God is with you, and you needn't fully understand God's plans or God's amazing grace. Just accept it."

"Thank you both," Samuel said, "your words mean a lot."

The two older men smiled. Without another word, they put on their helmets, turned, and mounted their commonlears. Zachariah said a quick prayer, and then their commonlears unfurled their wings and lifted off. Samuel, overcome with a newfound sense of God's mercy and courage, separated from the two seasoned veterans and veered toward Whiterock Castle. He felt as if a voice was ready to command his heart with each step along this perilous journey. It was freeing; it was convincing. God was speaking clearly and without judgment.

Jeff Miller

The wind swept briskly across the castle grounds. It nearly blew out Alicia's lantern. The returning soldiers hurried to get their commonlears into the stables for the night.

Alicia panicked. She could barely keep herself from calling out Philip's name. Trying to remain calm, she hurried among the troops and asked, "Have you seen Philip? Is he here? Where is he? Is he alive?"

"Yes, your majesty. He is alive and well," a knight answered from behind. She spun around. "But he is not here at the stables. He and Sir Jonathan had some business to attend to inside the castle. I believe they must be speaking with our future king regarding the outcome of the search."

"Future king?" Alicia asked.

"Yes, My Lady. King Donovan."

Alicia furrowed her brows. Resentment filled her eyes. "Sir, Lord Donovan is only a steward of the throne. Zachariah is the rightful heir until I am of age."

"Of course, My Lady." The knight bowed. "Please, forgive me." He rose and continued, "All of Sir Brendan's men died. We had separated into two teams in the event of a worgraith attack. They were ahead with the carriage when a worgraith came up from below them. It destroyed the entire group in a single ambush. But when we caught up with it, we were ready, with vengeance, and destroyed it. Sir Philip is a hero, My Lady. He led the charge and struck the killing blow himself."

The initial look of shock and horror on Alicia's face quickly shifted to admiration for her fiancé. She was relieved to know that not only did he come back to her safe and unharmed, but he had also been the hero of the mission. This reassured her that Philip was indeed a good man, the chivalrous man she had always known, the man to take care of her—and the man who was worthy to rule by her side.

"Thank you, sir," Alicia replied, softly caressing her pendant.

"My lady," the knight returned with a bow.

Alicia turned and headed toward the castle. As she neared the door, she noticed something small drift down in front of her. Snow? She looked up. She saw a thick blanket of deep, dark clouds. The wind picked up again. Could it be?

Alicia glanced about her but did not see anything else resembling snow. As she stepped forward and put her foot on the steps leading into the castle, something else caught her attention. She stopped and turned her head with furrowed brows. Alicia looked around some more. It seemed as if none of the knights or commonlears had noticed this peculiar anomaly. But there it was again.

It was a flash of light in midair, like a reflection off of a sword, just above the knights. Her attention turned to all the knights filtering out of the stables. She thought they acted odd for having just seen so many of their brethren slain. Not a single knight seemed to have mourned the loss of their fallen companions. Even the knight she had spoken to seemed a bit disingenuous. *What is going on?*

An icy wind raged through the canyon. Aiden had not spoken since he had seen the worgraith destroy the company of knights. He was angry. His father had tried, though, to say a few words, but to no avail.

King Jared, too, seemed distressed, and it was evident to Aiden. Angry thoughts boiled in Aiden's mind. The hatred that fueled a fire deep within him—a hatred for God, a hatred for Philip, a hatred for Donovan, a hatred for Xavier, a hatred for the way life had turned upside down. "There is no way out! Not even God could perform a miracle big enough at this point."

King Jared did not respond. He did not even look at Aiden.

"Alicia is to be sacrificed—maybe tonight—*maybe it's happening right now!* And we can't do *anything about it!* When I saw that troop coming, I thought maybe we could band together and stop it from happening. But now—*we can't even try!*" The lump in his throat wouldn't let Aiden continue.

King Jared spoke slowly. "And what about Samuel and Zachariah? Where are they? Are they part of this scheme, too? Will Whiterock ever again have an honest and noble king? And what about these worgraiths? I suppose Philip will continue to be their master. Then what? Will he use them to do his bidding, to subdue our kingdom and conquer our neighbors?"

"Father, are you…?"

"I'm—I'm *almost* without hope, Aiden."

"Father, let's face it. God has failed. Xavier has failed. Satan has won. This is *his* kingdom now." Aiden took a deep breath. His thoughts had exhausted him, as did all the events of the day.

Despite the anger, frustration, and fear swirling in his mind, he somehow managed to fall asleep quickly.

Alicia had searched the castle, trying to find a lighted room in the darkened halls.

"Alicia!"

She spun around. The castle's hallway was dark; she couldn't see, but she recognized the voice immediately. "I've been looking for you," she said. As he approached, the light from Alicia's torch brought him better into view. "Please, Lord Donovan, where is Philip? I need to see him."

"Philip? I don't know. I was about to ask you the same." A look of panic crossed Donovan's face.

"I saw the search party return without a hearse, and the numbers were small," Alicia said.

"Do you think he returned?" the lord asked.

"Oh, yes. He did. He's perfectly fine. I thought he might be with you. He wasn't to be found with his men."

"Then how do you know he's alright?" Lord Donovan asked.

"One of his men told me."

"Who? Which one?" he asked.

"I don't know," she said.

Lord Donovan's worry seemed to lessen. "Well, if you see him, tell him I'm looking for him, please."

"Yes, My Lord. I will."

"And I will do the same for you."

"Thank you, My Lord."

Lord Donovan smiled at her as if she were his own daughter. "Goodnight," he said tenderly.

"Goodnight, My Lord," she replied.

He turned and walked away into the darkness.

King Jared prayed in passionate whispers as he gathered wood for a fire. It seemed best to warm themselves as Aiden rested for a few moments.

The king slowly lowered his torch to the kindling, and thanks to just the right amount of wind at just the right time, it lit.

"God, is that You trying to tell me something about Your perfect timing? Because I don't know if I have enough faith to believe it just now."

As the harsh wind swept through the little camp, the diminishing fire resembled the king's diminishing faith. Eventually, he became too exhausted to focus his energies on prayer, and it wasn't long before the king lay down near the fire. "Lord, I don't know how to pray, or even how You can do this. But God Almighty… my faith is the weakest it has ever been. Lord, I don't see a way we can win, but… You must see something, You must know something, Lord, please…"

King Jared yawned. His eyes grew heavy. He tried praying more, but his mind could not concentrate. Eventually, as the winds died down, sleep overcame the exhausted king.

It wasn't long before two men slowly and silently walked out of the darkness, up to the fire, and with swords at the ready, stood over the sleeping king and his son. They motioned to the others.

"Come here, quick! You won't believe this! They're alive!"

Candles dimly lit a room that had been one of many out-of-the-way guest chambers. Sir Philip had ensured that while he had been away that night, his men had replaced all the interior furnishings. The great marble floors, walls, and ceiling were completely bare except for six golden candle stands and a golden throne upholstered with soft, black velvet. It sat on a round black carpet that had a golden five-pointed star inside a golden circle woven in the center.

Cloaked in hooded, black robes, Sir Philip and Sir Jonathan kneeled in silence with heads bowed and eyes closed as they invited their lord to appear. Sir Philip smiled widely as a faint smoke appeared. The smoke was sweet like a splendid mix of spices and flowers, but it was a scent foreign to anything found in or around Whiterock.

With eyes closed, Sir Philip sensed a wonderful, warm ray of light fill the room. Although the light diminished, the sense of a spiritual being in their midst intensified. It was a welcoming, almost teasing, addicting presence.

A clear, fluid voice spoke softly, "You may open your eyes."

As Sir Philip and Sir Jonathan did, their eyes beheld a beautiful man sitting on the throne in front of them. His skin shimmered like the gold on the throne. His black hair was long and straight and matched perfectly the black on his robe, his throne, and the carpet. Every feature of his face was strong. His eyes were as blue and clear as a summer sky, the whites of his eyes bright as a cloud. Those eyes held an unworldly power unlike anything Philip had ever seen or dreamed. It sent a chill down his spine. Lucifer looked as if he had been chiseled by a master sculptor. Everything about him was beautiful and perfect.

He smiled warmly. "I see you have obeyed my every command," he said.

"Yes, your majesty," Sir Philip answered.

"There are only a few commands yet left," the majestic lord continued with the utmost seriousness. "You must know not all of our plans have unfolded as I had originally designed. Our enemy has interfered. But do not worry. Only do as I command, and we will secure this kingdom as ours forever."

"Yes, my lord," both Sir Philip and Sir Jonathan replied.

"You must first release the worgraiths on the kingdom. Then, you will lead the charge against them. Do not worry how many of your men will die. You will vanquish the worgraiths as planned, I assure you."

The two servants nodded slowly in unison.

Lucifer held his head high. "Sir Philip, the people will forever remember you as the victorious leader who conquered the worgraiths after King Jared and Sir Brendan could not."

Sir Philip smiled.

"They will remember Sir Jonathan as the one who fought valiantly by your side. Sir Philip, your father must die so that you can assume the throne, crowned as Whiterock's greatest hero of all time. That is, *after* you sacrifice Alicia to me; do you understand?"

"Yes, lord," Sir Philip said.

"The sacrifice of innocent blood makes The Power Within strong," Lord Lucifer reminded. "As soon as you say the spell to unleash the worgraiths, bring the princess here. There should be plenty of time to sacrifice her before the worgraiths arrive. Tell your people that she and your father died in the attack. Now go. Your destiny awaits. The Power Within will be mightily on your side. We will fight with you to protect you and prevent our enemy from having a foothold against you."

"Praise you, wonderful Lucifer; The Bright and Morning Star," Sir Philip and Sir Jonathan said in unison, as if quoting a sacred liturgy. "You are mighty. You are wonderful. You are powerful in battle. Love, grace, and peace belong to Lucifer. He will reign forever."

Lucifer continued, "We will reign in all the world. There shall be no stopping the greatness of The Power Within. You shall have a seat at my right hand. You shall be glorified as the greatest servants of the Most High, I assure you. I promise your names will be glorified for all eternity!"

Lucifer laughed with great pleasure as he faded from their sight.

Sir Philip and Sir Jonathan sat motionless in awe and smiled, pleased to know that they were the most beloved of all of Lucifer's servants.

Samuel had never flown in such darkness before. The heavy, overcast sky hardly allowed him the fortune of seeing the snout of the very commonlear he was riding. The bitter temperatures at this altitude told him that winter was no longer looming; it had arrived.

But those were the least of his worries. He had to figure out a plan—how to find Aeric and Alicia and how to spread the news to the rest of the knights without drawing the attention of the enemy.

Enemy? he thought. *I'm not even sure who is friend or foe. How is that going to work out?* But he remembered his grandfather's and Sir Franklin's words. They truly believed that God had His hand on him. Something inexplicable was now telling him the same thing— something deep within.

Could God really have chosen me for something great? It's possible. But no, not me. I rejected God a long time ago. If God is real, then He would have surely chosen someone else by now. If God would have chosen anyone, it would have been Aeric. "But Aeric is dead," Samuel said in a hushed tone. "So, God messed up. He killed the very man He was going to use." Samuel shook his head.

"I'm not chosen. Not by You...*if* You exist. Who are You? Are You the God I've always thought You to be or not? I want to know. Show me. Prove to me You're not who I think You are. Give me something. Show me *clearly*." Samuel sighed harshly.

The unspoken voice he had felt earlier pressed into his spirit in a way that said, "Just watch." Within moments, through the utter darkness, Samuel could see the lights of the village at Whiterock. It was time to descend.

"I just can't believe you're alive. I watched you die." The astonishment in his eyes and a grateful, bewildered smile had not left Sir Brendan's face since he first laid eyes on his beloved King Jared and Prince Aiden. Sir Brendan and his men had gathered with the king and his son around a rekindled bonfire as the wintry breeze had settled down some more.

"And I can't believe you're alive, either," King Jared said. "We watched you die as well. At least that's what we thought we saw from here."

"What did you see?" Sir Brendan asked.

"We saw the torches fall," Aiden jumped in. "We saw the flames from the worgraith suddenly stop. It just got dark and quiet. I guess we assumed everyone was dead."

"No," Brendan said. He stared solemnly into the fire. "Actually, it was, in a sense, more tragic than that."

"You retreated, didn't you?" the king realized. "In such a manner that the worgraith wouldn't chase you."

"I've never had to retreat before, your majesty."

"You've never had to face a losing situation," the king said. "There are times to fight, and there are times to withdraw. This was the time to withdraw. You did the right thing."

"Then I shall swear to you; I will fight again. I intend to take my men back and seize Whiterock from Lord Donovan as soon as possible. But first, I want to know why. I don't want that man dead until I ask him why he betrayed his most excellent king."

"So, it is Lord Donovan, then? Not just Philip?" The king asked.

"I…I don't know exactly."

"We've assumed it, too," Aiden said. "But we just aren't sure, either."

"How…how could you have assumed? Did you find something out?"

Aiden answered, "Yes. We know everything—well, almost everything."

"How?" Sir Brendan inquired.

"Xavier," Aiden answered.

"Who?"

"Xavier," Aiden answered. "You could say he's a friend."

Samuel landed the borrowed commonlear in a wooded area close to the castle. The lights from the village were dim. It was almost impossible to gauge how to land in a blackened forest, but minus a few scrapes from the treetops and limbs on the way down, Samuel's commonlear landed in a small clearing just fine.

They followed what little light from the village they had available to them and made their way near the castle. The royal stables were not far, and Samuel still hadn't come up with a plan. He glanced at the regal commonlear. "Any ideas?"

It gave a somewhat hopeless snort.

"That's what I thought." Samuel let out a quick breath and said, "Okay, I say we find Alicia first and then warn the knights. That way, I'll know she's safe. I just hope I don't run into any unfriendly knights." He took a deep breath. "Let's move. There's no time to waste."

A pair of small candelabras gave out just enough light for the servant of Satan to perform his task. Large, bound books were open on a high wooden table in a compartment adjacent to the room in which Satan had just appeared. The small adjoining room had been a small den or library for whomever King Jared's guests might have been. It was accessible only from the former guestroom. The small circular space seemed a perfect place for Sir Philip to perform his assigned incantation, and later, it would serve as one of the many storehouses for the scrolls and other bound resources he would need for The Power Within.

Reading aloud words that were in a foreign tongue, not every word even fully known to himself, Sir Philip recited the incantation eloquently. Smoke and perfume arose from incense as Sir Jonathan meditated quietly in the center of the black carpet in the adjoining room.

Philip spoke more passionately, and it became apparent that he was no longer in control of his own speech. Although he had been reading the spell to summon the worgraiths, he closed his eyes and allowed The Power Within to take possession of his words. As he did that, Sir Philip let The Power take more possession of him—

his whole body, mind, and spirit. The more he released himself over to The Power, the more it increased in him. In all the years he had practiced this religion, he had never felt this much of its influence take control before. It was as if he became superhuman, a wild beast. He could do anything now.

As the spirit possessing him finished performing the magic charm, Sir Philip hunched his body over the books, hands firmly gripping the table, breathing loudly and deeply, almost snarling.

"The worgraiths—they're coming," he said to Sir Jonathan. "Now, let's find Alicia."

"Praise God. Praise God almighty!" Verbal confirmations resounded around the campfire as Sir Brendan's party finished hearing Aiden's account of meeting Xavier and all that it had entailed, including the charge to take back Whiterock.

King Jared spoke up. "I think we all need to praise God," he said. "Come, let us gather around the fire and sing His praises. Let us ask for guidance and direction. We mustn't make a move without His leading."

More confirmations resounded among the men.

"If indeed we are to take back Whiterock with force," King Jared continued, "we better make sure the Lord's battle plan is our own. Let us pray."

As the men bowed their heads, Aiden slowly and quietly walked away from the warmth of the fire into the bitter cold darkness. He found himself a bit surprised to utter a prayer of his own—one that wasn't filled with anger.

"God, I now know that You're real," he whispered. "And I can see where You have come through for us—keeping Sir Brendan alive—in a time that seemed hopeless. But I'm not fully convinced that I can trust You. What about Alicia? I need to know that she will be safe." His heart raced with fear. Aiden turned to look at the men around the campfire. They were now singing a well-known hymn.

"God, out of all the men in this kingdom—and any other— they are the ones I admire most. They're on Your side." He continued watching them worship for a moment. "Do they know something I don't? They've seen battle, hardships, death. Why do they still serve You? Why do they not hate You? They should." Their praises got louder. "They should have all the reason in the world to hate You as much as I." Aiden turned around and kicked a stone into the brush.

"If I am wrong about You, help me see the real You. Help me see You the way they do. I think I may have gotten a glimpse, but it's not enough." Aiden stopped. His mind reeled from all that he had gone through, all the things that had tormented his mind, especially recently. "I want to have the assurance that if I die in battle tonight or tomorrow, I will not experience that utter darkness that I felt in the cave—that feeling I almost even feel right now. Losing my mother has been horrible. But I never realized what it might be like to be separated from her, father, and Alicia for all eternity. I don't want that."

Aiden noticed he had started praying a little louder. He looked behind him to see if he had caught the attention of the knights. No. Good. He lowered his voice. "God, help me. I'm still so confused. You seemed good, then evil, and now...I don't know." Aiden shook his head again. "But I do know that there is a greater evil out there, and we need to fight it. We need to take back our kingdom. I don't understand why this happened, and that's been driving me crazy."

Aiden shivered. He looked again at the men around the campfire. "But I can set that aside for now if You just show me You truly are on our side and will help. I beg You, if You're good, do something. Show me Your goodness, and I will follow You. Show me You are not Who I thought You are." Aiden hung his head, shivered again from the cold, and turned to go back to the warmth of the fire. But before he took his first step, he heard a gentle voice.

"You've made the right decision, Aiden. I'm proud."

"Xavier?" Aiden asked quietly. "Where are you?"

"Turn around."

Aiden did, and there he saw the angel of the Lord. "I'm glad to hear you call me your friend," Xavier said with a warm smile. "I didn't expect that. Quite frankly, it means a lot." Xavier didn't seem quite as intimidating as he once had, nor did he seem quite so tall and glorious. He seemed…human.

"You've shrunk," Aiden said.

"Perhaps," Xavier said as his smile widened.

"So, you think I've made the right decision? I haven't made any decision, not really." Aiden stepped closer. "I'm just…I'm just tired of living this way, with all the pain and hurt and anger. If God is love—I want to know. I want to understand. I want that love."

Xavier studied Aiden for a moment. "And what if God isn't the loving God you're searching for?"

Aiden looked back at Xavier, puzzled.

"Well," Aiden said. "I guess I will move on. I guess…I guess I just let go of God altogether? I don't know, maybe not. Maybe I'll let go of what I've thought God to be. Maybe I continue pursuing Him until I see what they see." Aiden nodded toward the knights, still praising God.

"And that's the right decision. You will have your answer tonight, Aiden," Xavier said. "You will see God perform a miracle tonight."

"What miracle?" Aiden asked.

The angel of the Lord examined the sky and said, "It looks like it may snow."

Aiden didn't particularly care for the angel's response, but it seemed to be just like God to not give a clear and concise answer when Aiden needed one.

Xavier looked back at Aiden. "It's time to take back your kingdom, my friend. Let's walk. I need you to introduce me to your soldiers. I must convey some information to them."

"Oh, won't they be surprised to meet you."

TWENTY-ONE

The cover of darkness was just what Samuel needed. He and his commonlear flew from their lookout spot to the stables. When they landed, Samuel pulled a hood over his head and walked the commonlear coolly to the stable doors, keeping his eye on all sides.

"There's absolutely no one here," he said. "I think there's hardly even anyone around those camps. It's hard to tell, though. If they can see me from there, at least they can't make out who I am from this distance…I think. Okay, friend, listen. I've got to put you in here for the moment. I don't think I can get away with sneaking all over…"

Then, as if a voice inside him spoke, he received another course of action. Samuel thought some more. "Something's telling me to fly to her window, though. I can't explain it, but…" Samuel looked up. "It's dark enough," he whispered. "Maybe we can get away with it." Samuel looked around, exhaled, and said, "Okay, God. I'm going to take a chance. Make this work." Samuel mounted the dragon, and slowly and gracefully, with as little noise as possible, flew upwards and faded into black.

Alicia had almost drifted back to sleep when she heard clacking boots just outside her door. She perked up. "Who is it?"

"It's me, Philip," he whispered. "I didn't even have to knock. Are you still awake?"

"Philip!" Alicia jumped out of bed and lit some candles.

"My Lady, I know it is improper for a man to come to the door of a maiden, but I had heard you had been looking for me, and I thought I would…"

Alicia unlocked her door and cracked it open.

Philip smiled. "My Lady, I…"

Her heart lifted. He was himself again. She felt foolish for having let herself get so worked up by his outburst. "It's okay. I'm so glad to see you," she whispered. The darkness couldn't hide the twinkle in her eyes.

"I was wondering, if it's not too late, if you might care to join me for a walk?" he asked.

Alicia looked down, pretending to think for a moment, but she couldn't conceal her smile. She looked back up again.

"I will," she breathed. "Just give me a moment to get dressed."

"Of course," Philip replied.

Alicia closed the door softly. It didn't take her long to put on something decent and brush her hair. She walked outside her door with a lit candle in one hand. She took Philip's arm, and they walked down the stairs.

"No, wait," Philip said a tad forcefully, "let's go this way, up the stairs."

Fear blanketed her.

"What's wrong," Philip asked. "My lady, you seem hesitant. Are you alright?"

"I'm fine. Maybe it's just the darkness. I'm sure my candle—and you—will keep me safe." Alicia smiled.

"Are you still wearing the locket I gave you?"

The moment Alicia and Philip took their first step up the staircase, Samuel had successfully landed on Alicia's terrace with hardly a sound. The night was still so very dark, but he saw the lit candles in her room.

"That's good. She must be in there," he said to the commonlear. He dismounted, quietly made his way to her window, and tapped softly. Nothing.

He tapped again, louder. Still nothing.

He called her name. No reply.

Samuel opened her large, glass balcony door with a loud creak. "Alicia," he whispered loudly, "it's me, Samuel. *Alicia*, where are you?" Samuel stepped in. "Alicia." Samuel tiptoed to her bed. *Hmmm…It looks like she's been sleeping and had probably just gotten up.*

Samuel looked around the room. Noticing her door cracked open, he slowly opened it, stepped out, and stood for a moment. He looked upstairs—nothing but darkness. He unsheathed his sword. Samuel glanced down the corridor, and again, nothing but darkness. Then he peered down the stairs.

He backed up, gazed into the gloomy nothingness that ascended the staircase, and felt a tug in his heart telling him he should go there. *That doesn't make sense. There's nothing up there except guest rooms. Why would she be up there?* The tug in his heart became stronger. But Samuel shook the thought from his head and headed downstairs.

"We will fight with you," Xavier said. "If you see flashes of light like the shimmering of swords but do not understand what it is, that's us in battle, fighting alongside you against unseen demonic forces. Our part is to open the covering Satan's army has on Philip's men and make a victorious path for you. Men, the Lord has heard your prayers. And because of your diligent requests, the Lord has summoned a greater number of troops to fight with us in the heavenly realm. You will all see the *true* Power take hold tonight."

The men shouted in agreement.

"Do not fear your small number. For who can stand against you when all Heaven is on your side?"

The men shouted louder.

"Be strong and full of courage, for the Lord will make a way."

The men shouted with joy.

"Aiden, King Jared," the angel said, turning to them. "You need commonlears." Before the king and his son could utter a confirming remark, they heard two commonlears grunt. They looked over to where the sounds were coming from. Not far into the woods, walking just behind the knights' commonlears, two others walked from within the forest.

"I believe these two have found the way to their masters," Xavier said with a smile. "They have been lost." The leaves rustled a little more, and then two commonlears appeared from out of the darkness.

"Lucy!" Aiden yelled. "Father, look, Enoch!" Aiden nearly ran to his commonlear dragon and gave her a hug. "Where have you been, girl?"

King Jared laughed joyfully and put his arm around his faithful steed, patting him warmly. "So good to see you, old friend."

"Xavier?" Sir Brendan asked. "Where…where did he…go?"

"It is apparently time for the angel of the Lord to go about his business," King Jared answered. "And I suppose it is time for us to do so as well. Men, are you ready?" The men roared as they raised their swords in the air, ready and willing to serve their king in battle. "Then let us take back Whiterock—for God Almighty and His glory!"

As the men shouted again, a huge, menacing shadow floated above their heads. It was twice as large as any of the other worgraiths. Its slow, dark flight was like watching a great ship pass above their heads. Then, a fleet of worgraiths the same size sailed above them.

"Father," Aiden whispered. "What is going on?"

"My Lord," Sir Brendan said. "Xavier said nothing about this. Did he even know?"

"I don't know," King Jared replied.

"But Xavier promised us victory," Aiden said.

His father answered, "And I believe with all my heart that if God promised us victory, then we will have victory."

Jeff Miller

Twenty-Two

"Halt!"

"*Ohhh*…" Samuel stopped dead in his tracks. "Bryce, let me explain."

"Who are…"

"It's me, Samuel."

"Turn around," Bryce said in a slow, slithery tone.

"Bryce?" Samuel gradually turned. "You sound…"

Bryce was baring his teeth and drooling like a mad dog. He had his sword above his head, ready to strike.

"No!" Samuel raised his sword, which met Bryce's just in time. "Let me explain!" Samuel yelled.

"There is no explaining," Bryce hissed. "The king banished you for treason. I'll have to send you back to the king—dead or alive." Their blades met again. "Preferably dead!" Their swords clashed furiously. "I was disappointed to find out you survived the worgraith attack."

"That's a little harsh, even for you, Bryce," Samuel said, deflecting Bryce's angry strikes. "Would it satisfy you if I said that I am a ghost?" Another clash of swords.

"You will soon be a ghost!" the servant of Satan hissed.

"Good. You're just the person I'd like to haunt."

Bryce fought harder. His forward momentum forced Samuel to back up the stairs. Samuel tripped backwards. As if a set of unseen hands caught him, Samuel was pushed back up again.

Feeling this supernatural aid invigorated Samuel, and he took the lead of the combat, now pushing Bryce backward. "I don't want to hurt you, friend," Samuel said. "I only want Alicia."

"Ha! You fool, is that why you came? You stole the king's gold, and now you want to steal the king's daughter?"

Samuel fought harder, and when he saw the opportunity, he turned slightly, raised his right leg, and kicked Bryce in the stomach. Bryce fell. Samuel pressed the end of his sword against Bryce's throat. "If it comes to that," Samuel said. "I'm assuming, though, she'll come willingly. I'm trying to protect her. And if you truly care for what's best for the princess, then you'll put away your sword and help me."

"I don't suppose you've ever heard of The Power Within?" Bryce let out a low growl. "You see, we have everything under control here. There's no need to worry. She *is* perfectly safe—safe from treasonous slugs like you!" Bryce roared like an animal.

Samuel's heart pounded. "Isn't there anyone loyal around here anymore?"

"Only those who are loyal to The Power Within," Bryce answered. "All others are dead."

"Not me," Samuel said, "and what about those still camped outside?"

"They'll soon be dead," Bryce growled, "and so will you!" With that, Bryce hissed, swung his sword, and pushed Samuel's blade away from his throat. He lunged at Samuel.

Samuel darted, causing Bryce to overstep. Samuel regained a firm grip on his weapon and took advantage of Bryce's mistake. As Bryce turned to face Samuel, Samuel thrust his sword quickly into Bryce's stomach. Satan's minion tried with all his might to swing his sword at Samuel one last time but failed. As Samuel dislodged his sword from Bryce, the servant of The Power Within fell to the ground.

"I'm sorry, Bryce. You gave me no other choice…" Tears welled in Samuel's eyes. He truly hoped Bryce heard those last words. Samuel had only a moment to mourn before he heard a scream from two or three floors above him. *That's her!* Alicia screamed again, but it sounded muffled.

Samuel ran up the steps, trying to distinguish exactly where she was. As he ran, he also heard some scuffling sounds, some male voices, and more muffled screaming. As Samuel ran further into the darkness, he couldn't help but notice something strange at the top of the flight of stairs. He had just talked about ghosts, but…what was that on the landing?

It seemed as if there was a sword fight happening, but there were no sword fighters. All he could see was the shimmering of light as if there were unseen warriors in a battle—a battle just like the one he'd had with Bryce. Samuel came to a dead stop. He didn't know if he should continue approaching this anomaly. "What *is* that?"

There was another scream, louder this time. Then he heard a voice call out, "Get Alicia, you fool! She's run away!" It was Philip.

"Thank you, God! It's about time, but thank you, God!" Samuel ran up the stairs as fast as he could, right through the unknown lights.

By the time King Jared's band of men had reached altitude, a miserably cold, wet mush of rain and snow fell. The worgraiths were in the distance and had not seemed to notice the warriors following, nor had the king's army detected any worgraiths behind them. The commonlears were flying as fast as they could toward the giant monsters but were having trouble catching up.

If only we could do something before they get there, Aiden thought. *God, if we ever needed You, it's now. Please, I'm not worthy of Your hearing my prayer, but, if You can, for our kingdom's sake, please show Yourself. Do something. Let us catch up and be victorious before the worgraiths reach Whiterock.*

Alicia ran as best as she could in the blinding darkness. Her sense of direction was off. She knew Philip would spot her if she crossed within the glow of the window. She stopped, panting. Her throat was dry, and her lungs ached. She could hear footsteps closing in behind her but could not see how far away they were. Alicia let out a quick, involuntary cry, turned, and headed further down the black corridor.

WHAM! Alicia smacked her head against a column at the end of the passageway. She stumbled and fell backwards onto the ground. Alicia rolled her body closer to the wall, hoping to hide from whomever was trying to catch her.

For a time, she heard nothing. *Where is he? Dear God…* Straining to see in the dimly lit hallway, she tried to find the nearby staircase.

She heard the footsteps again, creeping near. Alicia tried as hard as she could to move toward the descending staircase without making a sound. Inch by inch, she crawled. Closer and closer the footsteps came.

"I know you're here somewhere, my love," Philip said. "Where are you? Why must you be afraid of me? I only want your name to be part of the story of the greatest kingdom in all of history. Don't you want your name to be part of an eternal glory?"

Alicia caught Philip's silhouette as he passed in front of the window.

Philip gradually and cautiously strolled ahead, his sword pointing outward to help him move in the darkness. He was apparently unaware of where Alicia was—for the moment.

Alicia backed herself against the banister and ever so slowly inched down the steps backwards, facing Philip.

Tap. Tap went the point of Sir Philip's blade against the wall. "Ah, I see we're at the end of the hallway. Where must you be hiding? I call upon The Power Within to guide me. Power Within, let me see her."

Alicia froze. He moved in front of the window again. She saw the silhouette of her hunter inch closer to her, his sword pointed down at her. "Ah, there you are!"

Alicia screamed. She bolted from her position, her hands still on the railing, and followed it down the stairway as fast as she could, only guessing where the steps were in the utter darkness.

She didn't get far when she soon felt two muscular arms grasp her tightly around the waist. Alicia yelled in anger. She kicked and thrashed her body.

"It's no use, my love, it's no…"

Alicia angrily yelled again. As Sir Philip held her up, she kicked her heels repeatedly into his knees. The fight nearly caused his knees to give out. Her furious wriggling forced him to drop her.

He shouted in anger as she continued to run down the staircase as fast as she could, down two flights into a lighted area.

Alicia ran from the stairs, down a hallway, and saw a commotion in front of her. Knights gathered, looking at something or someone on the ground.

"Please, help me! He's gone mad—please!"

"Stop her!" Sir Philip commanded from behind.

The soldiers turned at her and unsheathed their swords. Alicia halted abruptly. "Do not run away, My Lady. I do not want to harm you," a soldier said.

Alicia looked down and saw what the soldiers had been staring at—the body of Sir Bryce. She screamed again, tears filling her eyes.

Sir Philip caught up to her, out of breath. "Good work, men," he pulled both her wrists behind her back.

"*You!…you're* the one responsible for killing my family," she said. "Why?"

"For a kingdom of eternal glory. If it can't be done in the Kingdom of Heaven, then it shall be done in the Kingdom of Whiterock," Sir Philip confessed smoothly. "And you, My Lady, should be proud. You will have a very important part to play in all of this. Your name will be famous for all eternity. For without you, my dear, none of this could happen.

"Men," Philip commanded. "Help me take her upstairs."

"NO!" she screamed, trying to fight her way free of Sir Philip's clutches. The men inched their swords closer to her. She had no other choice but to give in. She was helpless. "No, God, no!" she cried. "God! Save me!"

Footsteps resounded from the staircase. Without looking to see who it was, Sir Philip said, "Ah, Jonathan. It's about time you finally caught up with us. Where have you been?"

"I've been looking for you," an unexpected voice replied.

"Samuel!" Sir Philip screamed in disbelief as he turned around. "I thought I got rid of you!"

"I guess another Power had a different plan. Set her free. Alicia's coming with me."

"Come and get her," Sir Philip demanded.

"As you wish," Samuel said with a smirk.

"You two grab her and come with me," Sir Philip commanded his troops. "I haven't time to waste. I have more pressing business to attend to. The rest of you, *get him!*"

Obediently, and with great delight, the three remaining knights did as their lord commanded. Samuel took his stance and readied himself for combat.

Alicia screamed in anger again and fought against her kidnapper's clutches, but it was no use. They dragged her away into the darkness.

Jeff Miller

Twenty-Three

The worgraiths had barely come within sight of the village when the commonlears caught up with them. The glowing streetlamps combined with the snow and haze created a deep, dark-red glow in the skies.

King Jared raised his sword in the air, and all the others followed suit. He pointed his blade forward and shouted, "For our God and our kingdom—*attack!*" The commonlears screeched as their riders roared a commanding cry. They split up to surround the worgraiths.

The worgraiths at the back of their formation faced their attackers full on with a terrible snarl, while the other worgraiths at the front of the line pressed ahead.

The commonlears had no trouble seeing, thanks to the lights penetrating the darkness from the village not far away. But the large worgraiths had trouble in this light distinguishing the direction from which their many small, fast attackers were coming.

Cling! Clang! Clash! Samuel accelerated as he struck one sword, moved to the other enemy, then on to the other. His eyes and reflexes were as sharp as his sword. Samuel kicked a knight down the staircase, where he hit his head hard against the marble and did not get up.

Samuel then swung his blade at one, moved out of the way of another, blocking his strike. The two knights, standing side-by-side, struck at the same time. He raised his sword and blocked both of them. He held their swords in the air just long enough to turn his waist and move his leg into position to kick them both with one side kick.

As they fell back against the railing, he lunged for them, striking both of them across their faces with his sword.

The advancing party of giant worgraiths moved closer to the village at Whiterock as their rear guard kept the warriors at bay. The red glow from the village harmonized with the fiery red and yellow flames that shot out of their mouths.

King Jared flew to Aiden's side. "My son, I've commanded Sir Brendan to lead the charge here. I need you to take my men to the forefront of the worgraith formation. They must not reach the village. You must set up a line of defense."

"Me? But father, where are you going?"

"I'm going to the castle. I need to find Lord Donovan and confront him." The king looked at his men assaulting the worgraiths; then without turning back to Aiden, he said, "Go, my son. Take charge of my men. God is with you."

"But, father, I can't."

King Jared turned and looked Aiden squarely in the eye. "You can. This is your destiny. You were born to command the kingdom and lead it in time of war. I know you can do this. So long as you have God, you have the *real* power within you. *He* is your power. *He* is your strength. Lean on Him and *not* on yourself."

"I…I can't do it… you've said so yourself: I'm not a knight yet. I've barely earned the right to even be on this mission!"

"Don't fear, my son. I will see you again; I know it. God is with us." Without giving Aiden another chance to protest, King Jared directed Enoch to the castle and flew off.

"Alright, God," Aiden let out a deep breath. "I'm trusting in You." His heart raced. "I have nothing else to lean on."

Aiden snapped Lucy's reins and dug his heels into her. He circled around his men and waved his arm, signaling them to follow. The front of the worgraith formation was just within reach of Whiterock Castle and the village.

It snowed harder. The air was becoming colder, the atmosphere a darker red.

Samuel followed the hallway where he last saw Philip and a castle guard carrying Alicia away. The darkness concealed any hint of where they might have taken her. "Dear God, I'm listening this time. Where are they?"

A shimmer caught Samuel's attention. It was the ghostly apparition that he had seen before. But this time, still not knowing exactly what it was, the still, small voice within him said to go to where he saw the flashes of light.

"This *is* a leap of faith," Samuel said. As Samuel ascended an almost completely dark staircase, a bell rang from somewhere within the castle. Then, he heard a trumpet. "A call to arms? What is going on? Whatever it is, the castle will be teeming with enemy knights in a matter of moments. I'm considered a traitor. I'm about to kidnap the princess, and everyone's possessed. This is not good."

The call to arms awoke Lord Donovan. As soon as he sat up in bed, a knock came hastily at his door. "Uncle, Uncle, worgraiths are coming to attack the castle! A whole slew of them, twenty or more!"

"Dear God!" Lord Donovan said as he jumped out of his bed. He found flint to light his lamps. "Jonathan, I will be out momentarily—as soon as I put on something. Tell as many as you can to not wait for me. I can't let the castle and villagers suffer the wrath of worgraiths on my account…" Lord Donovan did not hear a reply. "…Jonathan…Jonathan?"

Slowly, and without the slightest concern, Jonathan said, "Yes, Uncle?"

Lord Donovan turned around to see Sir Jonathan in the doorway with sword unsheathed. "Jonathan, why are you not doing as I say? For the sake of the kingdom, go young man. *Quickly!*"

Without a word, Jonathan slowly walked toward his uncle as a sinister smile crept across his face.

"Quickly! Go! What is the matter with you? Don't you understand?" Lord Donovan asked.

Something roared loudly above the ceiling, and then there was a mighty crash that shook the room. Another loud roar resounded from one end of the room to the other, followed by the sound of fire blasting through the air.

More growls and snarls. More crashes. Warriors crying out against the beasts. Lord Donovan could hear it all—and see it— through the windows of the king's chambers. The bursts of fire lit up the otherwise complete darkness. "Dear God, look what is happening!" Lord Donovan said, his back to his nephew. "We're doomed."

"Oh no, Uncle," Sir Jonathan said slowly. "*You* are doomed."

Horror filled Donovan's eyes as he slowly turned to face Sir Jonathan. "What…what are you…"

A loud slam came from the door to the king's terrace. "Lord Donovan, you shall not take my throne!"

Lord Donovan and Sir Jonathan both turned, bewildered. "King Jared! Am I dreaming?" Lord Donovan cried. "You're alive!"

"Alive and well," the king replied as he hastened into the room and unsheathed his sword, pointing it at Lord Donovan. "I have given you permission to watch over my throne, not to seize it from me. Now I have come to claim it back. I will take it by force if I have to!"

"What do you mean? What is going on? I think you misunderstand something," Lord Donovan said as he looked back and forth between King Jared and Sir Jonathan. "Please, help me understand…" Another loud crash like thunder quaked the king's chambers. "…is this all a bad dream?"

"Did you not create this chaos? Are you not the mastermind behind The Power Within?" King Jared demanded.

"I…what do you mean?" The Lord looked at his nephew, who peered at him with animal brutality, his sword extended toward his uncle.

Lord Donovan placed his hand on his forehead. Dizzy, he stumbled slightly. "Truly, I do not know what is going on here. King, you must believe me…help me understand."

"Certainly, we cannot have either of you on the throne," Sir Jonathan said. "It will be my pleasure to slaughter you both."

King Jared gazed at Sir Jonathan. As a worgraith slammed into the castle, knocking Jonathan to the ground, Lord Donovan quickly gained his senses. He ran to grab his sword hanging on the wall near to where he stood.

King Jared charged at Sir Jonathan. Their swords struck. "You shall not have my throne!" King Jared shouted at Sir Jonathan.

"The Power Within will rule this kingdom and eventually this world!"

"Your plans will fail you by the Power that is within *me!*"

"We will see about that!" Sir Jonathan struck his sword against the king's. Demonic control amplified the knight's youth and vitality. He struck the king's sword again. With three brutal hits, Sir Jonathan knocked it out of the king's hand and across the room.

As Sir Jonathan was about to thrust down a killing blow, a thunderous yell came from behind. Jonathan quickly spun around.

He hurled his sword back and forth, his strength more than a match for his aging uncle. King Jared ran, picked up his sword, and rushed toward Sir Jonathan, who spun around and, with large sweeps of his sword, easily repelled the blows from both the king and lord.

The two elders combined their efforts against the strength of the younger to stave off his advance. Another boom shook the castle, knocking King Jared to the ground.

Boom!

Roar!

Boom!

Sir Jonathan and Lord Donovan fell. Jonathan rose quickly to his feet, but before Lord Donovan could get up, Sir Jonathan knocked his uncle's sword from his hands and thrust down his blade into Lord Donovan with a menacing laugh.

He turned around. "You're next, king," Jonathan said in a ghoulish manner.

"Never!" King Jared shouted as another bellow from worgraiths echoed overhead. Flames surged from the monsters, and the ceiling caught ablaze. Sounds of men, commonlears, and worgraiths under full combat roared outside.

"Before I thrust my sword through you, answer me one thing," the king demanded. "Did Lord Donovan have anything to do with this? Was he part of The Power Within?"

"He was just a puppet," Sir Jonathan answered in evil delight.

While flames overtook the ceiling above, King Jared lunged at his once-faithful knight. Their swords clashed again as fighting escalated outside. "Your plans shall fail you tonight!" King Jared declared.

Alicia wiggled to set herself free. She could not budge from the clutches of her once beloved as he tied her to a makeshift altar. Worgraiths slammed into various places on and around the castle as the battle raged outside.

"This night," Sir Philip said, "we shall be victorious, and The Power Within shall reign on earth—all because of you, *my love.*"

"No!"

Twenty-Four

Aiden's troops tried their best to rein in the worgraith onslaught, and much to Aiden's surprise, the knights under The Power Within were striking against the worgraiths as well.

"My Prince!" Aiden turned toward the voice. "We were encamped behind the castle when we heard the call to arms and saw the worgraiths. We arrived as soon as we could get armored. Your majesty, it is such a tremendous pleasure to see you alive!"

Aiden looked about. Hundreds of soldiers now joined the fight against the worgraiths. Aiden felt a great weight lift from his shoulders.

"What would you have us do, your majesty?" the knight asked.

"Just fight the worgraiths," Aiden answered. "If any of Sir Philip's men attack you—fight back. Until then, the worgraiths are our chief enemy."

"Sir Philip's men?" the knight asked.

"Yes," Aiden replied. "Just do as I say. And tell the other men who are on the side of King Jared to do the same."

"Yes, Sire!"

A heavy white veil of reduced visibility even more and made the red lights from the village below look like smoldering embers. But that did not hinder the king's men from fighting the great beasts with all their might.

The servant of Satan hissed at King Jared. A voice not his own lashed curses at King Jared in foreign tongues.

King Jared breathed heavily. The elder met each strike, but his strength began to wane. As Jonathan's blow came down against King Jared's sword, a crash shook the king's chambers and threw King Jared to the ground. He saw Jonathan's sword come down again. Jared had just enough time to swing his sword in defense, knocking Sir Jonathan's blade aside. King Jared had just stumbled to his feet when the burning ceiling gave way and crashed down between him and Sir Jonathan.

The servant of Satan snickered gleefully as a taunting victory burned through his eyes. Jonathan darted out of the room, leaving King Jared trapped in his chambers surrounded by flames.

Sir Philip read the ancient liturgy written by Satan, which invited the prince of darkness to sit on his throne and witness a sacred human sacrifice prepared for him. The battle raging outside did not affect Philip's concentration in the least.

Alicia wept as the knight that helped drag her into the chambers and tie her to the sacrificial altar looked down upon her with demonic delight. The golden throne in front of the altar glowed, and a mist permeated around it. A beautiful, godlike presence overtook the room while a stunning perfume filled the sacred chamber. It seemed as if the commotion outside did not exist.

WHAM! The door crashed open and broke Sir Philip's concentration. The light and image on the throne dimmed as the smoke dissipated. Samuel had arrived.

With demonic hatred, the knight who stood guard of Alicia bared his teeth like a wolf ready to strike. He raised his sword and lunged at Samuel with a ghostly war cry.

The king's men continued to fight side by side with Philip's, defending the castle and village from the onslaught of the worgraiths. Philip's men showed more fear and hesitancy at combating these monsters than the king's, and thus the fiery worgraiths more quickly defeated them. Aiden couldn't make out who of Sir Philip's men was leading the charge. Aiden showed no fear, nor did any of King Jared's faithful knights.

The commonlears ripped and gnawed the worgraiths' flesh as the knights dug in with arrows and swords. "Aim for the eyes, men!" Aiden yelled. "Blind the beasts!"

Fire spewed from the worgraiths as they writhed in pain, enhancing the skies' treacherous glow. The defeated worgraiths flailed, some crashing into the castle. Others, being defeated above the village, crashed into homes and shops.

"This is not supposed to happen!" Aiden cried out when he saw the path of devastation. "God, what's going on? Xavier, can you tell me? God, *please* be with us!"

Ping—ping—ping. *Sleet?* A flash and a low rumble filled the sky. *That isn't the flashes of light Xavier promised, is it?*

There it was again, a sharp, bold snap of blue-pink light followed by a roar that bounced around the atmosphere. Is this a lightning storm? In a blizzard? Aiden looked at his armor. *Great,* he thought, *now we'll be targets of nature, too.*

The colliding blades continued to disturb Philip's concentration. Looking directly at the faint light that should have produced Lord Satan by now, Philip pleaded, "Do not leave me, my Lord. She is here! Here for you!"

Philip heard a shriek of pain followed by a thud on the ground. He twisted around to see Samuel, who returned Philip's stare with the wave of his finger, telling Philip come. He was next. But Philip just gave Samuel a menacing smile.

"Behind you!" Alicia screamed. Samuel turned and swung his sword. With the agility only a man possessed by a demon could muster, Jonathan leaped like a wild animal over Samuel. Jonathan quickly turned to face Samuel and attacked.

The two fought swiftly as Sir Philip returned hastily to his ritual. A light emanated from the solid gold throne once again.

The blizzard made it impossible for Aiden to distinguish the kingdom's men from Philip's men. But for the moment, it didn't matter. Both sides fought against the worgraiths while dodging the unpredictable lightning. "Come on, men," Aiden commanded his troops. "You've got to fight harder; be merciless!" And so they were. The worgraiths scampered back and forth in the dark, thick ocean of sleet. Aiden called out some more. "They're apparently confused by their lack of visibility. Attack them now before they regain a sense of their surroundings."

Several commonlears flew together against one beast. Fire penetrated the mixture of black night, white snow, and red glow.

BAM!

Streams of white-blue flashes channeled throughout the dense clouds.

BAM!

Electricity spiraled up and down a worgraith. A stream of electricity jumped in a long line from one worgraith to another via armored man and commonlear. The bolt stopped as quickly as it started as giants, man, and commonlear fell limply through the thick darkness.

For a moment, everything became dark and quiet. Aiden couldn't see a thing. He and Lucy just hovered there. "Everything's gonna be okay, gal." He petted Lucy. "Just…hold…here for a moment. Let's wait and see where they're coming from." She squawked. "I know, I sense it, too." Aiden lifted his sword. "It seems as if they're encircling us. Get ready to dart."

He and Lucy both jumped as they heard the roars and shrieks of worgraiths. Then, in the distance, he saw worgraiths lighting their own kind on fire. They screamed, plummeting to the ground. *What is going on?*

"Aiden, where do you need me?"

"Sir Brendan!"

"We've vanquished all of them back there. It was tough; I don't know if we could have done so without the storm."

"Same here," Aiden said. "And we have more troops with us. The ones camped out in the courtyard have joined the fight."

"Great! And I think this thunder-snow must be the miracle we've been waiting for," Sir Brendan said.

"I…I guess you're right," Aiden said.

"It must be," Sir Brendan said. "I've only heard of this, never seen it; it's so rare. And from what I understand, this happens only in early spring, not late fall. What about the village?" Sir Brendan asked.

"We still need your help over there. Worgraiths escaped our barricade. There's plenty of destruction…"

"I'll take my men there now. Don't worry," Sir Brendan said. "We *are* winning."

Aiden saw his father's chambers smoking. He flapped Lucy's reins, but the instant she responded, Aiden stopped her.

"No, Lucy, my place is here with these men. My father trusted me with this charge. I can't leave. My heart aches for him and Alicia, but…"

As the fire grew around him, King Jared prayed, "Lord, if this is how I am to die, then please, let it be quick. Don't let me suffer the agony of flames."

King Jared then saw, standing before him, a giant and glorious image of a man, nearly as tall as his chambers. His glory was so bright that it enveloped his facial features. With the openness of the fallen roof, a blast of cold, bitter wind swept into the room as the mixture of breeze and snow suppressed the flames long enough to allow Enoch to fly into the room.

"Go," the angel said. "I will open the flames as I opened the passageway for you to go through the waterfall."

King Jared ran through the flames as the parted, and he mounted Enoch, flying off through the gash in the roof.

Twenty-Five

Within a short time, the light emanating from the golden throne developed into a fully formed being. Satan's eyes narrowed on Philip. He gave his servant a sinister yet approving smile.

The fight paused as Philip's eyes fixed on his god. The evil master's eyes lit up. He slouched slightly, crossed his legs, and folded his hands on his lap as if the clash were just simple entertainment.

Sir Jonathan pointed his sword in Samuel's face. "You are powerless, squire. In a moment, we will sacrifice the princess, and we will have complete control over this kingdom."

Satan nodded for Philip to begin.

"No!" Samuel yelled as a surge of anger flared within. Sir Philip took hold of a large dagger. Philip was halfway across the room, and Jonathan was barricading Samuel's way with a sword.

As if someone gave him the words to speak, Samuel said, "I have a greater power, a power mightier than Satan. I stand by the power of God!"

Satan laughed. "You have nothing," he said from his throne. "You are more *mine* than you are *His.*"

"You are a liar," Samuel replied to the fallen angel. "I am His—I am God's! As of now, I am a follower of God Almighty!"

A haughty smirk came over Lucifer's face. "That doesn't frighten me, squire," he said coolly. "Enjoy your trip to meet your God. I have this kingdom. Philip, continue the sacrifice."

"No!" Samuel cried.

Just then, a blinding white light entered the room. A presence of peace and power like none other overtook them all.

"Xavier. *Hmmph.*" Satan rose from his throne and walked toward the angel. "I thought you might drop by."

"It has been a long time, Lucifer," Xavier pointed his finger. "You shall be thrown out of this kingdom as you were the Lord's!"

Lucifer snorted.

Samuel noticed the angel's glory was blinding Philip and Jonathan, yet Samuel could see clearly. He ran across the room and knocked Jonathan to the ground.

Samuel leaped onto the altar and sprung off of it, lunging toward Philip. Philip saw Samuel's shadow coming down through the light, his sword ready to strike.

Philip dodged out of Samuel's way, turned, and kicked Samuel. As he fell down, he saw Jonathan coming after him.

Satan pushed back his black cape, unveiling smooth, black armor. He unsheathed a golden sword and walked closer to the angel. "You've given my men a good fight so far," he said, "but once I annihilate you, and Philip sacrifices Alicia, this kingdom will be mine."

"A good fight? You've not become any better of a liar, that's for sure." Xavier also unsheathed a sword. "This kingdom is still the Lord's."

Satan gritted his teeth and charged the Angel of Heaven. As their swords clashed, lightning, a low rumble, and heavy smoke emanated from their swords. Satan roared, lunged, and swung his sword at Xavier's side. Xavier's whole body winced, and Satan let out a sinister chuckle. "Come on, show me what you got," Satan said.

Xavier composed himself quickly. "Certainly," he said. Swords crashed again as a harder boom and heavier jolt of lightning and more smoke burst from of their blades. As Samuel resumed combat with Jonathan, Philip snuck out of the way and found his dagger despite the blinding light and smoke, intending to complete the sacrifice. Philip swore as he noticed she was no longer on the altar; the ropes that had bound her were burned.

Philip screamed as he looked around; he could not see where she was. The mist that gushed forth from Xavier had now surrounded the room, hiding her.

Xavier's blows became greater, which, coupled with the glory that emanated from his sword, quickly forced Lucifer down to his knees.

"Master!" Sir Philip cried as he shielded his eyes from the radiance of God's mighty angel and watched his lord huddle and twinge in agony through the smoke. "Master!" He could do nothing to save him.

Then, with one final blow to Satan's armor, a mighty flash of lightning and a peal of thunder interrupted Samuel and Jonathan's fight. Satan had vanished. Xavier lifted his sword peacefully in front of his face and quickly drew it to his side, signaling the end of the fight. "They're all yours," he said to Samuel. Then, God's mighty angel and his radiant, blinding glory faded from sight.

"Samuel!" Alicia screamed from the doorway.

Samuel turned. An enraged Philip drew his sword and advanced on one side while Jonathan stood on the other. But Sir Jonathan surprised Samuel when he looked squarely at Philip, pointed his sword at him, and said, "This is your fault! If you had listened to me, we would have had this kingdom by now!"

"This is not my fault! It's his!" Philip pointed his sword at Samuel. "Kill him!"

"I'll deal with him in a moment," Jonathan said. "But I need you out of the way first. This is going to be *my* kingdom! This will happen *my* way! I will not let Lucifer down as you have. I will not disappoint him!"

"I did not let my lord down!"

Samuel backed up. Jonathan leaped at Philip with supernatural, animal-like force. Philip hardly had time to react, only scraping his sword against Jonathan's. Jonathan didn't hesitate and gashed Philip's arm, forcing him to drop his sword. Philip stared at Jonathan, who paced like a prowling lion. Then, Jonathan darted to Philip, who, defenseless, tried to run. Jonathan beat Philip violently with his blade.

Samuel backed up to the doorway, clutching Alicia as she hid her face from the horror. But Samuel knew he could not leave. He had to finish Jonathan once and for all.

Jonathan wiped Philip's blood off his face as he turned slowly to Samuel. "Now, it's your turn. *Come here*," he said.

Samuel walked toward Jonathan with calm determination. He stopped, pointed his sword at Jonathan and announced, "By the Power that is within *me, I* will defeat you."

Jonathan screamed, leaped at Samuel, and resumed their conflict. Alicia ran into the hallway and stopped, not able to watch and not able to run. Swords swung furiously as the worgraiths' screeching outside grew louder, when...

CRAASHHH! The wall collapsed, and the whole castle shook as a mighty worgraith collided with the chamber. Fire gushed out of its mouth and into the room as it plunged onward to the ground. Chunks of wall and ceiling hit Jonathan hard, throwing him to the floor. The freezing blizzard breached the room, barely preventing the flames from becoming a massive blaze.

Jonathan stood, but not soon enough. Samuel attacked before Jonathan could regain his footing. Jonathan flung his sword in place to counter Samuel's blows, but Samuel's pace was too quick and forceful. Jonathan recovered his stance and started fighting hard again, trying to back Samuel up. But Samuel stepped forward and struck harder with every blow.

Samuel hit Jonathan in the wrists, which forced him to drop his sword in agony. In the blink of an eye, Samuel struck Jonathan in the chest and watched his body slowly go limp and fall, but an image of Jonathan remained standing in place.

This transparent likeness stood as if it didn't know its body had just died. Jonathan's ghost stared at Samuel, still wondering what had happened. Then, in shock, Jonathan looked down at his own corpse.

Suddenly, an eerie, wretched, angry, vaporous image of Philip materialized next to Jonathan. Philip hunched with fists clasped tight. His nose scrunched as drool dripped from his clenched and crumpled mouth. His eyes were flaming embers. He panted like a rabid dog, his clothes tattered. Philip pounced on Jonathan, and the two fought each other with their bare hands in bitter anger and hatred. Then the two images faded from sight.

Samuel turned, ran to Alicia, and they embraced. "What was that?" Alicia asked. "Their spirits?"

"I suppose so," Samuel said.

"Then, that's their doom?" Alicia asked. "Chasing and fighting against each other in hell forever? Their souls never to rest?"

"I don't know," Samuel said. Green smoke escaped the charm around Alicia's neck like a snake slithering out of a hole in the ground. Samuel reached behind her and unlocked her necklace. The castle shook as plummeting worgraiths battered the fortress. "Quick," Samuel said as he threw Alicia's necklace on top of Philip's remains. "Let's get you out of here."

Aiden's men continued flying to every worgraith they could find. Except for the occasional flash of lightning and streaks of white-blue bolts that struck the giant creatures, the dark, stormy atmosphere prevented Whiterock's army from seeing all the worgraiths at once; and no one could tell just yet how many they had vanquished or how many remained.

After a low echoing thunder that seemed to last forever, the snowy night suddenly quieted. Aiden could only hear the whooshing of Lucy's wings as she hovered in the empty, cold, dark night sky. Aiden peered around to gather his bearings. Though the sleet seemed to stop, the snowfall was still thick enough for him to not see well.

A sudden chill raced up his spine. He felt the power and wind of an enormous presence ascend into the murky sky behind. He turned to look. Lucy felt it too, and she moved around to face it head-on. Then, the shadowy presence drew closer, almost swimming in the ocean-like depths of the thick, black atmosphere.

As if in slow motion, Aiden and Lucy watched the beast as it came their way. They could see the shadow open its mouth as a ball of fire pierced the darkness. Flashes of light caught Aiden's attention. Small flashes, whirling in the air like the shimmering of blades.

"The angels!" Aiden said aloud. Then he regained his focus—and so did Lucy. Both darted out of the way of the killer beast. The worgraith discharged a giant flame into the darkness, where they once were.

Aiden and Lucy flew to the worgraith's stomach.

Lucy turned herself and her master upside down and dug her claws into the monster, which cringed as she tore mercilessly into its skin. Aiden gashed his sword into it as well, chopping it as quick and severely as he could. The worgraith took its monstrous hands and batted Lucy and Aiden from its belly, which caused Lucy to rip into the worgraith even more.

As it took a hold of Lucy, Aiden plunged his sword into the beast's hand, which caused it to open its grasp. Lucy darted off, straight toward the monster's throat. Aiden readied his sword, lodged it into the worgraith's throat, causing it to withdraw in pain.

Lucy rammed into the beast's throat again as Aiden repeatedly sliced it with his sword. The worgraith again instinctively swung its hand at his attacker, but before it could, Lucy moved out of the way, around the monster and to its neck. There, she allowed her master the opportunity to lodge his sword into the giant dragon precisely where its skull met its spine.

It shuddered in pain, stiffened, and then fell. As it plunged downward, quietness blanketed the kingdom again—but only for a moment. Aiden then heard the sounds of men and commonlears in the distance near the village.

Jeff Miller

Jeff Miller

Twenty-Six

As the golden-blue light of daybreak struggled to penetrate through the white, stormy haze, Aiden spotted the silhouette of a small army flying on commonlears. "Lucy, who is that?"

She snorted.

"Oh no, let's hope it's not more of Philip's men."

As Aiden drew closer to the battle over the village, the morning light helped Aiden see his men keeping the worgraiths at bay.

Aiden dug his heels into Lucy's sides and commanded her to move. Within moments, the band of men and commonlears that Aiden had once seen in the distant horizon arrived at the battle scene about the same time as he.

"Sir Franklin! Zachariah!" Aiden said.

"Aiden!" Zachariah said. "Where is your father?"

"I don't know. He went to find Alicia. I haven't seen him in quite a while."

"Alicia?" Zachariah said. "Samuel should have found Alicia by now. You haven't seen him?"

"No," Aiden said. "I had no idea where he was—or that he was even in any condition to do anything."

"Who's been leading this charge, then?" Zachariah asked.

"I have."

"*You?*" Sir Franklin asked. The two elders smiled.

"Well done," Zachariah said, beaming. "Well done." Without another word, Aiden, Zachariah, and Franklin joined the army of lords as they all moved forward into battle over the village. As the snow lessened, dawn brightened the sky, revealing King Jared's approach with Enoch.

"Father! Father, you're alright! Where's Alicia?"

"I don't know. I've been looking frantically for her. Have you seen Philip or Jonathan?"

"No, not at all," Aiden replied. "I heard Samuel has been looking for her, too. Hopefully…" The two sensed flames behind them and veered their commonlears in opposite directions to avoid a worgraith fleeing from noblemen.

Aiden waved his arms, signaling the knights to lure the worgraiths outside the village boundaries. The men did as their leader commanded, leading the worgraiths in a game of chase to resume the fight in snow-covered fields away from the village. Jared caught up with Aiden, and the two fought side by side.

With the skies over their homes safe from the fire-breathing dragons, the villagers came out to the wells and formed a bucket brigade to douse the worgraith fires.

High above the ground, commonlears soared all around the immense creatures who could not keep up with the onslaught of so many small, harsh, and determined foes. Invigorated, each knight battled as the dawn brought hope to a brand-new day.

One by one, the worgraiths fell, and then, two by two and three by three—downward-spiraling, slamming hard into the snow-covered ground. The storm ceased, and the sun shone brightly in a majestic golden sunrise. Quietness blanketed the atmosphere. The men looked around. There were no more worgraiths.

A loud, rousing cheer erupted from the villagers below, breaking the peace of the moment. The knights soon joined in the celebration.

King Jared flew Enoch closer to Aiden. "I am proud of you, son; so proud. You have proven yourself a great leader."

"Thank you, Father. You were right. Not just about me, but… about God. He did come through, didn't He?"

"He did."

Inspecting the damage in the village was the knights' first priority. Aiden could hardly walk anywhere without someone coming up to him to bow down and express their gratitude, praising him and telling him what a great king he would be someday.

"Thank you!" one old man said. "Thank you so much. Oh, God has been good to us! He has spared us from those terrible monsters."

"Tell me," Aiden asked. "Where do you live?"

"Oh," the man replied. "I—I used to live there, but the worgraiths' fire destroyed my home. Oh, thank God you were here!"

"The fighting nearly destroyed the village. Your home is gone. People died, and yet you're not cursing God?"

"Oh, no," the man said. "How could I ever curse God? God gave us victory just as He had done before. Whiterock has not been delivered into the hands of those beasts—as some other kingdoms have been in times past. God should be praised!"

Aiden was speechless.

"Thank you," the man said again as he bowed. "Thank you so much. Praise God!"

Aiden graciously said farewell and walked along some more. He saw people help others to the village's recovery center. Neighbors worked to gather remnants of each other's belongings, and amidst it all, people praised God for their victory over the worgraiths.

"What are you staring at, brother?"

Aiden instantly recognized that voice. "Alicia!" Aiden spun around and saw his sister running up to him. Her hair was a windblown mess, and her skin had the evidence of a few scratches, cinder, and soot. But despite everything, she was in good spirits.

Alicia stretched out her arms and squealed joyfully as she stomped through the snow in her fur-lined leather dragon-riding boots. She gave her brother a hug and squeezed him so hard it hurt. "I'm so glad to see you!" she said.

"I'm so glad you're alive! Father's been looking for you. We both thought you were dead. Tell me," Aiden said. "Where *were* you? What happened? Did anyone try to hurt you? You look fine…"

"I'm more than fine," she said, smiling. "Thanks to this man right here." Alicia turned to the young man approaching from behind with a young commonlear in tow.

"*Samuel!*" Aiden shouted. "What happened to you? Where have you been? I imagined you'd still be in the infirmary. Look at you!"

"I've been busy taking care of a few things. You know, like battling demon-possessed lunatics, having tea with Satan. You know, just a few small things."

"*You've what?*" Aiden asked.

Samuel smiled. "Well, let's just say Philip won't be bothering us anymore. He got his wish, though. He's finally in his lord's eternal kingdom. But from what I can gather, I don't think the experience is going to be exactly what he thought."

Aiden was speechless. Samuel returned his stare. Then the two blood brothers smiled at each other and laughed as they embraced. "So, did you hear about the rest of Philip's crew?" Aiden asked.

"No," Samuel answered. "Where are they?"

"It seems from our record of survivors that all our men came back alive—without a single scratch. Philip's men, however, all died. All of them. And *just* them. But listen, none of us fought against Philip's men. It just so happened that they all died from worgraiths; and the worgraiths happened to only kill Philip's army. What's more amazing is that the worgraiths seemed to be more or less blinded by the snowstorm, so they had no apparent ability to distinguish who they were killing. They couldn't have just chosen to only kill Philip's men; it just happened that way."

"Or so it seemed," Samuel said.

Alicia added, "That shows you that God was fighting the battle."

"I think I've seen quite a few miracles that have proven that," Aiden admitted.

"And so have I," Samuel said.

"Listen," Alicia said. "I have to find Father and let him know I'm alright. Where is he?"

"He's at the castle, assessing the damage there," Aiden said.

"Is my grandfather with him? I need to let him know I'm all right, too," Samuel asked.

"Yes," Aiden said, "they're both there."

"Great," Samuel replied, "and thank you."

"Thank you? For what?"

"For what you did last night. I'm impressed. The entire kingdom is talking about you, you know."

Aiden looked at the ground.

"I guess some knights just started talking about your leadership and…"

Aiden shook his head.

"Soon they'll be talking about you, Samuel," Alicia said, taking his arm.

Aiden smiled. "I suppose so. But exactly what will they be saying?"

"I'll tell you all about it." Alicia said.

"Fine, over tea; just don't invite Satan this time," Aiden said.

"Oh, trust me," Samuel chuckled. "I won't." With that, Samuel and Alicia flew off on Aeric.

As Aiden's eyes followed them to the castle, the view from where he stood confirmed that it was in near ruin. It would have to be rebuilt, no doubt, but enough of it survived that it was probably in livable condition. It was still beautiful, even in this state. Aiden turned around and walked some more. He saw knights and squires gladly lending their aid to the villagers wherever they could.

He walked outside the village boundary to a hilltop overlooking both the community and the castle. The morning's warmth brought a beautiful fog over the pristine, snow-covered valley and above

Spring Creek. It was only a few days ago that he had seen a similar sight—before the snow had fallen—while there was still autumn in the air. It's hard to believe just how much had changed in such a short amount of time.

Yes, how much had changed—only a day ago, Aiden would have blamed God for the destruction he saw in front of him.

"God, you've shown me more than I thought was possible," Aiden said. "You've shown me You. You've shown me that You care. You've shown me that You are good—and that there is another force out there working its evil."

Aiden walked some more, soaking in the view of the snow-covered landscape in this light. "You've shown me where I was wrong. And You've shown me that having all the answers isn't what it's all about. It's about You. It's about being in a right relationship with You. It's about letting You show me Your mercy and love."

Aiden turned around and started walking toward the castle. "Instead, I've just blamed You, hated You, and yet You pursued me to show me I was wrong, that You are not who I thought You were." Aiden stopped, sighed, and hung his head. "Forgive me for all the hatred and bitterness that I've had against You. I will not let it ruin my life anymore. I'm Yours."

A giant weight that he did not know he had suddenly lifted from his spirit. Aiden felt peace and joy burst in his heart, something he had never felt before. The presence of God filled his soul. He felt as if he had been made new, as if he had been born all over again.

About the Author

Jeff Miller

Jeff Miller is the pastor of First Baptist Church of Watkins Glen, NY. His sermons can be found on kingdomwinds.com, and you can follow his two blogs at: acloserlookjm.wordpress.com and flashbackfridaychristianmusicreview.wordpress.com